THE REALM

THE FABLE OF MORALITY

I. MICHAEL GROSSMAN

PUBLISHER'S INFORMATION

EBookBakery Books

Author contact: imichaelgrossman@verizon.net

ISBN: 978-1-938517-99-0
Library of Congress Control Number: 2020936322

1. Morality 2. Ethics 3. Religion 4. Faith

"*The source of inner joy is to be in truth.*"

- Paraphrased from a talk by the Dalai Lama XIV on *The Art of Happiness*

ACKNOWLEDGMENTS

Our lives are so busy. Which makes me all the more grateful to the following who took time to help me create *The Realm.*

Thanks to Dr. Sal Abbruzzese, Bill Azano, Nancy Azano, Pastor Clay Barry, Ken Dautrich, Dot Distel, Enid Flaherty, Gene Kincaid, Camilla Lee, Susan Mandel (*my partner and wife*), Lenore Maroney, Jane McCarty, Dr. Gene McKee, Yvette Nachmias-Beau, Terry Schimmel and Peter Stonberg. Special thanks to Jim 'JT' Transue for his eagle-eye.

Tracy Hart (editingwithhart.com), my editor, has once again shown her ability to identify missing pieces in the puzzle of a plot; to note a poor choice of words and offer better ones; and to urge me to cut a phrase when, as excess baggage, it isn't worth it's weight in ink. Again, I'm the lucky recipient of her amazing talent.

DEDICATION

To all of us struggling to be better, sometimes falling short.

CONTENTS

PREFACE

I think increasingly about ethics - or more specifically about how they impact us. I've known students who are okay with cheating on tests if they can get away with it. There are athletes who dope or deflate footballs and celebrities who bribe to get kids into elite schools. A few senators ignore the constitution to stay in office, and even the courts, the last refuge of ethics, arc politically.

I'm not saying it's worse now. Our ethical standards have always been in question, and maybe things are better now. But whether we're more or less moral isn't my focus. I'm interested in the psychological impact of our values.

The Dalai Lama is clear about what happens when we abandon truth for gain. The price is diminished happiness. We're less joyful and not so self-content.

Despite prosperity, I suspect we aren't history's happiest people. Speaking for myself, I've spent more than one therapy session wishing for a do-over because I didn't live up to my moral aspiration. I'm not talking about big stuff - robbing banks. I'm thinking of tiny transgressions - like moments at a party when I should have stood up for an unpopular person or cause, but I wordlessly sauntered away. It didn't feel good.

I'm no one to proselytize. As a kid I stole candy from a store. (Mom made me return it and apologize to the manager.) I once cheated on a physics test (and still nearly flunked!). I'm guilty of my share of moral weakness.

But this is also not about guilt. There's more than enough of that around. Instead, it's about how to feel good.

As I age, the thing that's strengthened me most - that makes me feel the most good about myself - that comforts and even brings me joy - is when I do the right thing - act morally - when I'm a straight shooter and I don't opt for a convenient lie.

I'm trying hard to be ethical for selfish reasons. Because it makes me feel wonderful. Thankfully I've reached the point these days when I can look in the mirror and feel happy about the old guy staring back. He makes me feel joyful.

I wrote *The Realm* to fictionalize this issue - to take it to the nth degree in a world where immorality not only rules but is high virtue - a Sodom and Gomorrah where meanness is worshiped. As is power. And ruthlessness.

How do you succeed in such a world and should you? *The Realm* suggests the dilemma, and hopefully points the way out of Hell.

I. Michael Grossman

1

MIRACLE DRUG

Edgar Wormwood tapped his ear. *Forgot my hearing aids, dammit and probably missed Attorney Thaddaeus's call.*

His hearing aids were on his upstairs nightstand which meant climbing eleven stairs that loomed like the Matterhorn.

His heart struck a double beat. Arrhythmia. *Shit, I forgot my heart meds also.* The climb was no longer optional.

He stretched for his cane, sending pain through his rotator cuff. Swollen joints and stiff muscles added discomfort as he thump-shuffled to the stairs. He held the handrail at the landing to catch his breath.

Sitting on his bed, Edgar fingered back thinning strands of hair to fit the hearing aids. Trembling hands didn't facilitate the task, but he succeeded in time to hear the phone ring. Downstairs. Repeatedly.

"JoAnn said I should get a cell phone," he muttered. "I would if I could work it."

♦

JoAnn entered his bedroom later that morning, leaning to gently kiss her father's forehead. "Did you hear yet from Jim Thaddaeus?" She sat beside him on the bed.

"He never called."

JoAnn raised her eyebrows. "Were you near the phone?"

"I had to come up here."

"How about we see if Thaddaeus is still in his office before we miss his deadline?" she asked.

"Bet he figures we'll lose anyway or he'd have called."

"I bet he did call, Dad, it's a class-action suit. He can't coddle a hundred clients. Let's go downstairs and try to reach him."

Stairs, thought Edgar.

Edgar was an early patient on the Olaphane regimen, a new anti-inflammatory approved to combat the throbbing muscle pain that tormented him. Though he didn't offer a formal diagnosis, the orthopedist believed his symptoms warranted Olaphane, recently released by Lexamin Pharmaceuticals.

Initially Olaphane provided noticeable relief, and within weeks Edgar was taking the stairs with comparative ease.

"Look at you, Dad," JoAnn had said as he ascended. "You're doing great."

◆

It would have been wonderful had relief from the drug lasted. But in a matter of months Edgar began experiencing joint stiffness again and pain even greater than before. Movements turned leaden as nerve stabs spiked his shoulders, arms, hips, finally reaching toes that became unresponsive. Shins tightened like a vice and oddly, his voice started to gravel.

He wasn't alone. JoAnn pointed to an article in the *Boston Daily Journal* noting other patients on Olaphane were reporting a resurgence of symptoms. Several had to be hospitalized complaining of angina. The *Daily* quoted an orthopedist who hypothesized that Olaphane reduced the flow of oxygen in the blood to the heart. Two of the hospitalized patients suffered heart attacks and didn't come home.

Edgar's doctor's solution was, "I'm going to double your dosage."

"Seriously? Double my dosage? That's the best you've got, Doc?" said Edgar. "I'm sure the drug is my problem and that's your solution?"

The doctor continued to write the prescription.

"You know what, Doc, I'm outta here," said Edgar, dragging himself out of the exam room.

Edgar's next stop was to St. Francis of Assisi, his church, to pray for relief with Father Angelos. "It's in the hands of our Lord, Edgar," said the priest, gently touching Edgar's shoulder. The black beads of his rosary rolled over the priest's hand as they knelt. "God always has a plan."

Later, Edgar mailed a vitriolic letter to the Massachusetts Board of Registration to denounce his physician as incompetent. The letter timelined his experience on Olaphane, the progressive suffering, and referenced the *Boston Daily* article. When weeks passed without the courtesy of a reply, an angry Edgar went further.

His call to FDA headquarters in Silver Spring got voice prompts to a recording that assured callers how seriously the administration took its role as public protector. A second lengthy trail of prompts led finally to a human who listened as Edgar described his experience on Olaphane with references to the *Daily Journal* article.

"I'll pass your comments on, Mr. Wormwood," said the manager. "Thank you for sharing. Can I help you with anything else?"

"Will I hear from anyone or is this it?"

"Oh, surely you'll get a reply."

♦

After weeks without one, Edgar called the FDA again, demanding to talk to a higher-up. A string of transfers led to the First Secretary to the Administrative Assistant of the Director of the FDA's Center for Drug Evaluation and Research. *Jesus, how does she get that on a business card.*

"We are looking into this; make no mistake we are, Mr. Wormwood," said the secretary. "These things take time."

"Time, Ms. Whatever-you-said-your-name-was, is what I don't have."

"It's Evelyn."

♦

Sitting with Edgar at the dining room table, JoAnn shoved aside his stack of unpaid bills and edged closer to her dad. "Let's call Thaddaeus again," she said as slender fingers tapped her cell phone. JoAnn lowered tortoiseshell half-glasses as the speaker-phone broke the silence. "Teaberry, Thaddaeus & Rabine," said a receptionist.

"Wormwood," said Edgar. "For Thaddaeus."

"Good afternoon Mr. Wormwood. Attorney Thaddaeus is in court. We tried to reach you this morning. Will we be getting your signatures today?"

"Never got your papers," said Edgar.

"Our messenger left them yesterday, sir. When no one answered your door. I left you a voicemail as well?"

"Never got it," said Edgar.

"Ask her to hold, Dad. Let me check the porch," said JoAnn.

"Wait. We're looking," said Edgar drumming fingers.

"Here they are," said JoAnn placing a flat envelope before her father. "They must have been out there all along. Sign them and I'll call for a messenger."

"They're on the way," said Edgar leaning into the speakerphone.

"Thank you, Mr. Wormwood. I'll let Attorney Thaddaeus know."

◆

Six months earlier, JoAnn came after mass to prepare Sunday breakfast for her dad. Both looked up when "Olaphane" was mentioned in a TV commercial. "I'm Attorney James Thaddaeus," said the spokesman. "If you or a loved one is a patient on Olaphane, I urge you to call my office." A series of symptoms scrolled below with an 800 number and the promise of operators standing by. The commercial finished as Attorney Thaddaeus, rows of leather-bound books as his backdrop, promised "no legal fees are paid unless damages are awarded."

JoAnn offered to call.

"It won't go anywhere," Edgar said. "What's the likelihood that a bunch of patients can take on Lexamin Pharmaceuticals?"

"Dad, the commercial says it's free so what's to lose?"

"Call if you want, Jo."

The operator at Teaberry, Thaddaeus & Rabine confided nearly a hundred patients had called, all reciting Olaphane side effects.

Soon afterwards, Edgar and JoAnn met with a Thaddaeus paralegal, and, after also consulting Father Angelos, Edgar signed the papers to join the class action lawsuit.

◆

Edgar made another call to the FDA, this time transferred to the Secretary to the Director of the Office of Pharmaceutical Quality. She listened as Edgar complained that the FDA's drug evaluation procedures were lax, and it was too easy for a drug like Olaphane to get approved.

"Not really, Mr. Wormwood," said the Secretary. "Our drug trials are extensive and take years." She summarized FDA drug approval steps.

"All well and good, but it didn't take them years for Olaphane."

"Actually it did, Mr. Wormwood. Lexamin submitted several years of trial history with data documenting reductions in pain and symptoms."

"... yeah but they lasted how long?" said Edgar. "A month? Two months? I'm in agony. All of us are."

"There will be anomalies," said the Secretary. "But the results from each of Lexamin's four standard trials, evidence statistically insignificant side effects."

"Ah, so I'm, what'd you call me, 'an anomaly.' I hope your children don't grow up to be 'anomalies'. What I really am is a Guinea pig. You have no idea how Olaphane wrecked my life and the lives of my fellow 'anomalies'.

"I'm sorry to hear that."

"Meanwhile, Lexamin stock goes up and you at the FDA sit mute. I'm a taxpayer. We pay you for drug scrutiny."

"Which we provide..."

"...since you don't get it, let me speak to the Director himself."

"She's not available. Would you like her address?"

♦

"Dad," said JoAnn, holding the receiver, "It's your roommate Terry from the hospital. I'll put him on speakerphone. Ask if he's any better since he stopped Olaphane."

Terry Harkness and Edgar had shared a room when they were hospitalized with similar symptoms after taking Olaphane.

Terry, a fifty-four-year-old husband and father of two girls, had been able to resume work and get off disability after starting Olaphane. But following a brief period of relief, his pain returned and became overwhelming. He had to quit work again and go back on disability. Money was an issue, and to help pay the mortgage, Terry's wife took a job. They postponed corrective leg surgery for their daughter, knowing they couldn't cover the co-pay. Terry also joined Thaddaeus's class action lawsuit, his last hope for solvency.

"... this morning," said Terry, "... Ralph ... at Mount Sinai. Ralph was only 48. His wife told me the doctors called it 'paralysis of the nervous system.' Poor bastard's heart seized."

"Jesus. Does Thaddaeus know?" Edgar asked.

"Just got off the phone with them," said Terry. "They sent the firm's investigator to the hospital for Ralph's medical history, assuming she can get through the HIPPA wall. Ralph has two kids, ya know."

"Rotten," said Edgar. "What about you? Pain any better now that you're off it?"

"Not much," said Terry, "the damage is done. To be honest, it's spreading. Feels like I'm dragging stone to walk. Same as you."

"I wish I could say it gets better, Terry." Their conversation paused.

"See you at tomorrow's prep for the trial?" said Edgar. "But call me sooner if you find out when Ralph's funeral is."

"How long was Ralph on Olaphane?" JoAnn asked when Edgar hung up. "Maybe you and Terry stopped soon enough?"

"You seen me walk lately, Jo?"

JoAnn turned away.

♦

JoAnn took a sip of tea at dinner with her dad a week later, then opened the top bill in the stack on his dining room table. The *CANCELLATION PENDING* stamp across the electric company's bill was hard to miss.

"I'm taking this, Dad," she said, folding the invoice.

Edgar snatched it back.

"You have to have lights, Dad, for God's sake."

"My pension check comes tomorrow. I got it."

"I just want to help."

"You've done enough already, JoAnn. Do you think I don't know you canceled your new Camry? And postponed my granddaughter's orthodontia. The kids come first. They're exceptional girls - even if I wouldn't recognize them without an iPhone stuck to their nose."

"You really have this thing about technology, Dad."

"I suppose I'm old fashioned enough to think people should talk to each other instead of texting. Terry told me kids on a date are texting each other."

"Fine, but you're not changing the subject. You need basic services, and I'm not letting you go without them." She snatched back the electric bill.

"You're awfully good to me, Jo, but think of the kids."

JoAnn knew it was useless to protest further.

2

BOARDROOM

Soft overhead lights lit the marble corridor leading to the Lexamin Pharmaceutical conference room. Executives chatting at the long rosewood table fell silent when Director Andrew Kapinski entered. Rhoda Esterwood placed folders in front of him as he took his seat at the head.

"Lots to cover today," said Director Kapinski, sliding the folders closer. "Let's get to it. Rhoda, start with the current sales environment."

"Of course, sir. Good morning all. So as predicted, the numbers are softening. We're down in the West especially with second quarter Olaphane sales off 22%."

Gene Carry, responsible for West Coast sales, straightened his tie.

"Across the board, sales have dipped 18% - all regions combined," Rhoda continued. "Olaphane issues are getting national coverage after that *Daily Journal* article put a spotlight on them."

Kapinski glared.

"But on the positive side," Rhoda hurried to add, "the announcement of the new Physician Inducement Plan is gaining traction. Enrolled doctors already show significant increases in prescriptions and are on a path to reach their targets. It's just a matter of time before Lexamin stock gets a bump."

Kapinski's frown softened.

"In two months, maybe sooner, we'll see a spike." Rhoda eyed him. "Of course, that assumes the FDA falls in line."

"Which brings us to the Hill?" Kapinski turned to his right.

Emmit Rashovi smoothed back his hair, set his coffee aside, and reached for his chart. "The lobbyists have high confidence HR1035 will pass which gets the states $920 million in new prescription support." To highlight the uptick in commitments from the House, Rashovi tapped a tall column in blue on his chart, using his Montblanc as a pointer. "Alabama's Latislee and Arizona's Finderly sent letters to the FDA's Gronstein to prompt for his promised support. We expect the funding to get to the states before the term is out."

"Levine?" Kapinsky looked down the table at a balding man with wire-rim glasses. "The research? How strong is our case that Olaphane isn't causing the problems patients report? How many have another medical diagnoses we'll argue is the root cause of paralysis? Have we identified them in sufficient numbers?"

Darius Levine, the Director of Pharmaceutical Research, read from notes. "In all, 47 patients exhibit appropriate pre-existing conditions, representing 7.2% of the symptomatic population. This percentage is certain to increase before their lawsuits reach the circuit courts. Our attorneys are assembling each patient's medical history. We'll make a compelling argument factors other than Olaphane caused their paralysis."

"How long has the FDA had our new research?" asked Kapinsky. "What's their response?"

"Not yet, sir. They don't have it yet. We need a month to complete it." Levine tried to smile.

"Goddammit Levine, I want it to them now. I'm not letting this thing snowball."

Levine looked down at the table.

"As to a trial," Kapinski continued, "should Judge Batchelder deny our motion to dismiss, I want the most articulate of those 47 patients primed to make our case at trial. I want convincing testimonies from them that will shift the jury's focus off Olaphane." He hard-stared Levine. "I want the jury to feel sure, beyond doubt, that preexisting factors in each patient's medical history led to their hospitalization; that the etiology of their ailments isn't pharmacological.

"Yes, sir."

"Of course, patients who support us will enjoy our gratitude."

"I believe that's also being taken care of, sir," said Levine.

"I don't want 'belief,' Levine. I want assurance."

◆

Judge Batchelder of the 6th District court denied Lexamin's dismissal motion and set a trial date. Attorney Thaddaeus for the claimants met with Lexamin's attorneys to hear their perfunctory settlement offer. Just as routinely, Thaddaeus rejected their low-ball bid and advised his clients by letter of the upcoming trial date.

◆

Edgar's phone rang the week after he got Thaddaeus's letter.

"Mr. Wormwood? It's Mariam from Teaberry, Thaddaeus & Rabine. Attorney Thaddaeus is wondering if you have a moment?"

"Sure," said Edgar. *The big gun himself.*

"A moment please, sir."

"Edgar, Jim Thaddaeus. An okay time to talk?"

"Sure, Jim."

"You feeling any better?"

"I wish I could say I was, but the pain gets worse by the week. Like the others from what I hear."

"Yes, and I'm sorry Edgar. I'm afraid I am hearing the same from your fellow litigants. It's the reason for my call."

"Okay?"

"You know the trial begins on the 14th?"

"I do."

"I'd like you to testify."

"Me?"

"You can help."

"What can I do?"

"Forgive me, but I'm going to be blunt. I want the jury to see how bad things are for you. When I call you to the stand, it'll be obvious you're in agony. I'll ask you to describe what life is like these days: your symptoms, your suffering, your loss of mobility - the cost of being unable to work."

"I get to be a poster boy for the glories of Olaphane, huh … me and a few of the others, I suppose?"

"As I said Edgar, I don't mean to be insensitive, but you dramatize the drug's problems."

"Jim, let me ask you something."

"Of course."

"What are our chances? Can we win? I don't mind admitting I could use the money. You must think we can or the firm wouldn't take it on contingency."

"I think we have a fair shot but no guarantees. We're facing Lexamin, a deep-pocket bunch, as you know. But jurors are human, and when they see you take the stand, you and a few others, I think it will sway them."

"I suppose all of us can use the money." Edgar eyed his stack of bills.

"Yes."

"Suppose we win. What's it worth?"

"Jurors are mercurial, Edgar, but I believe, in time, a substantial settlement is possible. I won't speculate on how much."

"I suppose it's unfair to press, but say the jury finds in our favor. Whatever the amount, what kind of timetable are we looking at?"

"We have two goals, each with a different timetable. Do you mean how long before a litigant gets compensated? Or, how fast can we get Olaphane off the market?"

"Paid," said Edgar.

"If the jury finds for us, we have every chance of getting Olaphane off the market in a matter of months. We must. The drug's a killer."

"It won't be hard to convince Ralph's widow of that," said Edgar. "She's raising two kids alone now."

"Exactly," said Thaddaeus.

"But I'm asking about getting paid?"

"I've never misled you, Edgar. I think we have a solid chance the jury will find for us. But the bottom line is, we're dealing with Lexamin. They won't roll over if they lose. They'll appeal and drag it on. In the end I think we'll win … and pretty big. But to be really blunt again, Edgar, you don't have years, and I'm truly sorry for that. But it will benefit your daughter JoAnn."

3

THE MEETING

Weeks later, Edgar, having remembered his hearing aids, heard the phone ring.

"My name is Thomas Loki, Mr. Wormwood. Might I have a moment of your time?"

"Tom who?"

"Thomas Loki, sir. I have information you'll want to hear."

"Sure you do. I don't want a loan; I already have cable, life insurance, magazine subscriptions and all the credit cards I want. How about not bothering me," said Edgar, moving to hang up.

"It's news about Olaphane. News you'll want to hear."

"How do you know I'm on Olaphane?"

"I wonder if we could meet? Briefly," said Loki. "I'll come at your convenience. There are Olaphane developments that make the conversation worth your while."

"I asked how you know I'm on Olaphane."

"I'll explain when we meet."

Edgar pressed for details, but Loki wouldn't provide them over the phone, insisting on a face-to-face. Edgar thought about dismissing Loki, but during their conversation the man evidenced an in-depth knowledge of Olaphane symptoms. *Is he a sufferer too? Loki seems clued in on the upcoming trial. Does he have information I can use?*

"If we meet," Edgar said, "I'd want someone from Thaddaeus"s office present. And maybe Father Angelos."

Loki would only agree to meet alone, saying his information was privileged. Something in Edgar's gut urged him to go ahead even on Loki's terms. *I can always involve Thaddaeus's people later.*

◆

Loki arrived, a slight man in a precisely-tailored wool suit, carrying a full-grain leather briefcase. Edgar showed him to a seat at the dining room table but asked to skip the pleasantries and get to it.

"I'm not in Lexamin's employ," Loki began, "but occasionally I do projects for Darius Levine, the Director of Research for Lexamin."

"I've read about him," said Edgar, "and I wondered if you were associated with them. I'm sure you're aware that I'm represented by council. Why aren't you talking to Jim Thaddaeus?"

"I'm a physician, not an attorney. Nor am I on Lexamin's staff. I'm here as a favor to Levine," Loki said. He spoke in a voice with words that seemed to echo.

"So you're Levine's friend. From what I've read about him, I didn't know he had one," said Edgar, raising his eyebrows. He again considered sending Loki away, but curiosity won out.

"You know I have nothing positive to say about Olaphane, Mr. Loki. Or about Lexamin for that matter. So what's Levine want with me?"

"May we discuss your medical history?" asked Loki, pulling a folder with Edgar's name on the label from his briefcase.

"You have my medical records?" said Edgar. "How in hell did you get them?"

Loki smiled.

"You've had early onset Parkinson's symptoms, Mr. Worm-wood," said Loki, moving his finger along sections highlighted in yellow. "They were first noted a decade ago - all the major indicators: difficulty walking, calf weakness, stiff muscles, the telltale tremors of head and hands."

Edgar looked surprised. "So?"

"Of course you're on Thaddaeus's list of witnesses for the claimants, and Lexamin will cross when you're called."

"We're getting into legal matters," said Edgar. "I won't go there without someone from Thaddaeus's office present."

"You can be a hostile witness," Loki continued, "or friendly."

"I have nothing 'friendly' to say about Olaphane. I'm a cripple thanks to it, for Christ sake," said Edgar.

Loki's finger tracked several dates on the medical report. "Your Parkinson's symptoms exhibited seven years before you started on Olaphane."

"And your point is?"

"So your suffering stems from Parkinson's, Edgar. Olaphane has nothing to do with it. Preexisting conditions account for every one of your present difficulties: your muscular stiffness, the tremors and paralysis. Any doctor knows they indicate Parkinson's. And Parkinson's is typically preceded by a decrease in dopamine levels which makes signal transmission neuronally encumbered. Your history," Loki tapped the folder, "shows you evidenced that decrease besides having the other Parkinson's-related symptoms. Parkinson's is what ails you."

"What a load of crap," said Edgar. "You expect me to call this," he raised his trembling hand, "a preexisting condition? I may have had a few of those other symptoms for years but not this." He held up his hand again. "This began two months after I started taking Olaphane. None of my doctors ever suggested Parkinson's."

"It is Parkinson's, Edgar. You have it and have for years. You should be willing to say so and support people who benefit from Olaphane."

"I should lie? For Lexamin?"

"Lexamin isn't asking for anything more than that you accurately confirm your medical history. Only the facts," he said, waving the medical report. "Surprise testimony can be persuasive at a trial."

"Surprise testimony?"

"The element of surprise is powerful. Dramatic. You'd be expected to keep our meeting confidential until the trial … until you testify."

"You're serious? Because you're nuts, Loki, if you think I'm getting up there and saying anything that supports Olaphane. Lexamin's made my life a nightmare … mine, Terry Harkness', Ralph's, may he rest in peace, and a lot of others. You do know about Ralph?"

"Unfortunate. But Lexamin will prove he also had Parkinson's."

"Crap," said Edgar, trying painfully to rise. He reached for his cane. "We're finished, Loki."

"In fact, Edgar, your medical history evidences how well you did on Olaphane - until your Parkinson's reversed its benefits."

"Bullpucky."

Loki, remaining seated and held up his palm to halt Edgar. He tapped the ever-present stack of unpaid bills on the table. "I understand medical difficulties aren't all you're facing," Loki said. He pulled another folder from his briefcase, flipping papers page by page. "Electric, phone, mortgage, credit cards …"

"You have copies of my bills too?" Edgar sat down.

"Your mortgage is past due … long past. They started eviction proceedings. Where will you live? With your daughter who paid your last heating oil bill? Will you move in with her family when the bank forecloses? Or don't you think she …," Loki glanced in the folder to be sure of her name, "… don't you think JoAnn has enough on her hands? A single mother with children. Your grandkids."

Edgar's chest sagged.

"… furthermore, you need treatment for your Parkinson's and you can't afford it," said Loki. "You exceeded your insurance coverage seven months ago …"

Edgar took a weary breath, then turned to Loki, "What are you suggesting?"

"The folks at Lexamin are dedicated to public health. They've expressed their concern for you, specifically. They feel your mortgage and other expenses shouldn't be a source of stress on a man in your condition, and they'd like to help."

"With a bribe I assume?"

"Lexamin doesn't do bribes. But they are conducting a study of Olaphane users … on the effects of preexisting conditions. Patients receive substantial remuneration to participate in the study that confirms Parkinson's is at the root of your present symptoms. The study will make that conclusion evident at the trial."

"You have others lined up to testify?"

Loki smiled. "We want nothing more than for you to confirm your medical history when we cross examine you. We're asking only for facts; that you tell the court what Parkinson's has done to you."

"Testify on Lexamin's behalf? For Olaphane?" Edgar shook his head.

"Think about it, Edgar," said Loki. "They want nothing more than the truth." Loki stuck the folders in his briefcase and rose. "Let me know, and thank you for meeting with me."

Edgar stared at him.

Loki's eyes held deliberately on Edgar's stack of bills before he turned to go. "Suppose I call tomorrow?" his voice echoed as he left.

Edgar sat. *I have a right to keep my home. I worked for it my whole life, and it's not my fault my medical bills are pulling me under. And I can't keep piling my troubles on JoAnn. She'd never tell me, but I know she's behind in her own bills. But testify in support of Lexamin?*

I can't do that to Thaddaeus, to the others. Lexamin's attorneys will quiz me about each Parkinson's symptom, one by one, and I'd have to acknowledge I had them. Suppose Thaddaeus can't make the jury see I wasn't incapacitated until after I got on Olaphane? Lexamin is a powerhouse with teams of lawyers. Look how easy it was for Loki to get my medical history and copies of all my bills.

I have to pray on this and ask Father Angelos for help.

◆

Edgar studied his eviction notice. He had a month to come up with the mortgage or lose his home.

Do I go along with Loki? Apparently Lexamin has other patients lined up. But Thaddaeus won't know what hit him. It isn't right. Terry Harkness ... Ralph's wife ... they'll all be sunk, and I'll have to look Thaddaeus in the face when Lexamin cross examines me.

4

IN GOD'S HOUSE

Father Angelos offered Edgar a chair. A charcoal sketch of the 'vicar of Christ,' Pope Gelasius, hung on the wall behind his desk next to a simple wooden cross.

Edgar lowered himself awkwardly to take a seat.

"Pain any better, Edgar?" he asked.

"Not really, Father. Bending isn't easy."

"I'm sorry, Edgar." Father Angelos, still in his vestment from mass, said nothing for a moment as he took in Edgar's condition. "And JoAnn? The children?"

"Doing well, Father. Her finances are tight thanks to me, but her health is good. Actually it's about JoAnn I've come."

"How can I help?"

"I need your guidance, Father, perhaps more today than even when Rosemary passed, although I still don't understand why God took her so soon."

"Rosemary was a wonderful wife, and I still picture your face the day you came ... so full of loss. I hope I was of help."

"You always are, Father, and I'll be forever grateful. But today I'm flailing again. I'm tormented by a dilemma I don't know how to handle."

"Tell me, Edgar."

"Forgive me, Father, but I have to speak in generalities ... for your protection."

Father Angelos's brow furrowed.

"It's an issue of survival but it's complicated because there are other parties involved. Some will get hurt - me or others." Edgar paused.

"Yes?"

"Surely, God would want me to keep my home, wouldn't He?"

"Is that threatened in some way, Edgar?"

"It's a financial dilemma. And a moral one. One choice means I lose everything - including my home - and I place an even larger financial burden on JoAnn. My daughter insists on looking after me. There's another choice that spares me financially. But I'll have to harm some perfectly innocent people, many of whom have become friends. How do I even approach such a decision?"

"The devil's in the details, Edgar, and you haven't given me any."

"There are legalities, Father, and I don't want you involved."

"Isn't there a way to protect both your daughter and your friends?"

"I don't see it, Father, and believe me, I'm struggling for an answer. Either I'm ruined and take JoAnn down, or I harm the others. I can't find a middle ground."

Father Angelos paused, the dim light of the room casting shadows under his eyes. "I want to help, but it's difficult to guide without information. Our conversations are privileged, of course, Edgar."

"It's to protect the church, Father, that I shouldn't say more."

Father Angelos swiveled in his chair. His eyes fell on the wooden cross as he paused in thought.

"Suppose we approach this from a different angle," said the Father. "Is there a moral consideration? Is it more ethical to do one thing or the other? When I'm faced with a decision like yours, the difficult choice arises from the reality that there are no simple black or white answers. As children, right and wrong was simple to decipher. Steal a piece of candy or don't. Go to bed on time or refuse to. But as adults in a world that grows more complex, crowded, globally enmeshed, it's rarely that simple. Solutions are intertwined with compromise, and satisfying all parties is so much harder. When I'm faced with decisions like that - I recall Matthew 7:13-14."

'Enter by the narrow gate. For the gate is wide and the way is easy that leads to destruction, and those who enter by it are many. For the gate is narrow and the way is hard that leads to life, and those who find it are few.'

"Is there a narrow gate, Edgar?"

"That's what's so hard, Father. My gate is wide or narrow depending on how I choose to see it. I want to do the ethical thing. I want to be able to feel good about myself, see someone I'm proud of in the mirror, but I don't know how to get there."

"Alright." Father paused. "Does either choice cause you to break Christ's commandments? Lead you to steal, commit adultery … tell a falsehood?"

"I don't actually have to lie to save myself. I could state the truth in a way that's not lying. But I wouldn't be completely truthful either; and in my heart, I'd know I had deceived."

"There you go. Then the choice is clear, isn't it, Edgar?"

"Not as clear as that sounds, Father. Because if I follow my heart, that's when I lose my home and drag JoAnn down. My daughter's stretched to the limit now from paying my expenses."

"Then God has given you a bewilderment, hasn't He? Without more specifics, my answer can only be that you do as I do in such a case, and ask for His help. I think of Mark 11:24."

"Therefore I tell you, whatever you ask in prayer, believe you receive it and you will.'"

"You think prayer will offer me direction?"
"I do and if you like, I will pray with you."

In the dim of his office, Father Angelos spread his vestment so he could kneel beneath the simple wooden cross. Edgar followed and they bowed heads in silence.

Father Angelos arose after a time. He explored Edgar's eyes hoping for clarity but he saw only a bewildered, lost child of Christ. Father led the way through the nave, and Edgar left the church.

5

POST LITIGANT

The afternoon following the trial, Edgar got up from the dining room table. The table was clear, his stack of bills gone, and, cane in one hand and a glass of Glenkinchie in the other, he made his way to the porch for his favorite Adirondack chair. He took a deep pull of scotch, enjoying a brilliant orange sun as it lowered at the river's far shore.

They did a hell of a job preparing me for testimony, he considered, *though I feel horrible about blindsiding Thaddaeus, a decent man.*

He'd taken his lawyer by complete surprise. Thaddaeus called Edgar to the stand, expecting to capitalize on Edgar's labored walk, ready to quiz him about Olaphane's painful side effects.

But, as practiced with Lexamin's physical therapist, Edgar walked to the stand with apparent ease, concealing his pain. He'd practiced suppressing the grimace tied to movement so that for all appearances, the side effects Thaddaeus just described to the jury were a sham. The Lexamin attorney followed and in machine gun fashion asked Edgar a series of questions confirming Edgar's medical history that showed evidence of early Parkinson's. Edgar, avoiding his fellow patients' eyes, replied in the affirmative as the lawyer listed symptom after symptom. A few in the room gasped.

Often seated on the porch as twilight set, he would think of Rosemary, and his spirit would slide. Thirty-seven years and then she was gone. The house echoed silence, and he kept her side of the bed made though blatantly empty. He hated how self-conscious he felt shopping alone for groceries or sitting at a restaurant table with a single place setting.

While Rosemary was still alive but slipping, he remembered how irritable he'd become; how he snapped at her nurses as the cancer ate away at her and they seemingly did nothing. She grew thinner - then a wig - the nausea following infusions. He'd wanted to slap the heavyset nurse who took several tries to insert the needle into ever-thinning veins. The slow drops from the plastic bag that hung above her, dripping poison crudely intended to destroy cancer faster than healthy cells ... but killing both.

At least Rosemary didn't live to see him testify. He'd pleaded with JoAnn who, despite protests, finally agreed not to come to the courthouse. He couldn't face seeing the pride in her eyes dim. She'd learn soon enough what her dad had done. At least he was no longer a financial burden. *Aren't fathers supposed to support kids, not the other way around?*

Edgar grabbed his right arm. The stabs of pain were sharp and came more frequently now. "Doubtless 'preexisting Parkinson's symptoms," he muttered sarcastically.

He eased deeper into his chair and took another sip. But the pain spiked, sharper now and it burned across his chest like molten lava. He had to pull for breath. His body spasmed, and eyes locked as he stiffened, motionless.

JoAnn found him there in the morning.

◆

6

DEARLY DEPARTED

The moment his heart stopped, Edgar was reborn. He regained what seemed like consciousness, though it was confusing and came with the sensation of spinning, slowly at first, then reaching a pinwheel pace. He rose, seeing his earthly body below slumped in the chair, the glass of scotch spilled on his pants. His vision clouded, akin to the blur seen by a child peering through a strip of cellophane. The sense of motion continued but it was difficult to contextualize, to translate into a familiar reality. It was as if he was 'hearing' motion, experiencing transition as humming like the buzz of an electric wire.

His ability to distinguish up from down was gone, and lateral movement was also indiscernible. He thought of astronauts in zero gravity, but it wasn't that either. Frantic, he pawed to grab something, anything. The concrete realities he relied on for grounding had abandoned him.

He forced himself to hold it together, to pause and take measure. He would reason this through - think rationally, redefine, translate it into terms he could recognize. He'd start at the beginning and follow sensations in sequence. That would place him, get his bearings. But try as he did, it wasn't possible to regain the familiar. He'd come untethered.

What was that sound? That hum again? Or was he hearing color, listening to the patch of gray falling over him? It grew darker, louder, then turned a deep black. Was he entering a cave? A womb?

7

THE REALM

Edgar's transmutation continued. He felt like he'd fallen through ice and desperately flailed for an edge, something to grasp that would stop the sense of sinking.

He passed through a whirlpool of sparks that left him frantic for physicality - for the feel of flesh and bone. Had he taken a new form? Was this 'spirit'? Yet even as he hungered for corporeality, his material disassembly continued and spread through his systems - his nerves, cardiovascular paths, musculoskeletal structure, lymphatic and respiratory organs. One after another each organ dissolved into a river of milky molecules, turned into a thousand grains of sand floating on a viscous stream.

He lacked a sense of being, of existence, history, time - there was nothing more and nothing less than black tunnel walls, themselves transitioning, flickering.

The loss of feeling a body kept him adrift until finally he sensed a slowly, returning solidity - as if the thousand grains had passed through a filter and reassembled out the other end. Had he come to rest? *Is this my destination?*

Edgar reassembled in the Realm of Paradox.

Sensations previously felt through his body now came as vibrations. Yet he felt solid. It was all so contradictory. *How can I be light as a feather while solid as a rock? This has to be an impossibly vivid dream,* Edgar concluded. *There can't be a place like this.*

He could no longer dodge the question.

Am I dead? Yet I'm still processing thoughts. And the sense that I've traveled is so real.

Attempts to understand proved futile, and he simply let go, submerging in the experience without further struggle. As he gave in, his panic subsided.

Floating … he had a sense of floating. It occurred to Edgar that this place, the curious virtual-like world he'd entered, would require a new openness, a vulnerability to the experience. Caution, native to Edgar's nature, was earthly and tied to his fear of mortality. Alive and embodied, he avoided risk. Now abandoning caution was a relief. He tried to relax into it as a virgin gives in.

With his willingness to be there fully, came an awareness of another presence. His sense of it grew and with it came a flush of warmth, a feeling of sunburn, though he had no flesh.

"Edgar Wormwood."

His name reverberated.

"Wormwood."

Without eyes, he could not search, yet Edgar intuited the communication came from a similarly disembodied spirit. It seemed close and very real. Lacking a body, Edgar could only think a reply. He concentrated, drilling the simple word repeatedly through his thoughts, "Yes? Yes?"

"I've been waiting, Edgar. Welcome."

The communication came as vibration, as unsettling as hearing his name.

"Who are you? Where is this?" Edgar concentrated a reply.

"You're anxious, Edgar, and you needn't be. I am your escort, here to ease your transition. That you're disoriented is expected, but have no fear."

"Escort?"

"'Guide' if you prefer. To help you acclimate as we prepare for your Justification. I'll be taking you to the Chamber of Justification. It's where, when you are ready, you'll appear before the Chief Magistrate ... for *your* Justification."

"I don't know what in the hell you're talking about."

"Exactly, Edgar. But now we must go."

The dark tunnel pulsated with colors as Edgar accompanied his self-proclaimed 'escort'. Lacking physicality, he simply "intuited" movement, still attempting to translate it into earthly experience, equating his passage to the view out a subway window.

"I feel dizzy. And it's so dark, guide. I'm completely lost. Where did you say we're going?"

"You're confused. We all were. We'll briefly visit the Chamber of Justification. That's the most important stop on the tour. Our unholiest chamber."

"Huh?"

As if tectonic plates shifted beneath his feet, Edgar was carried into what he interpreted as a vast arena. He sensed other points of consciousness focused on him. He was surrounded by vibrations, as if hearing a hundred conversations.

"Edgar," another entity greeted.

Edgar felt a difference instantly. This entity's vibration was intense, bold, harsh like static compared to the gentler vibrations of his escort.

"Edgar Wormwood."

It's not easy adjusting to how they communicate. He concentrated, *"Yes?"*

"He's here to begin?" The entity's vibrations seem to crowd Edgar. "Did you cover the requirements for Justification?"

"Oh no, Lord Dambalah, sir. He's only just transitioned from the embodied. I haven't even started to prepare him," said the escort. "This encounter was unintended."

"Justification? And what in the name of God is this place?" Edgar felt slapped, hard.

"Never use that word," said his escort. "Especially not before our esteemed Chief Magistrate."

"Never indeed," boomed the harsher entity.

"But, who are you, sir?" Edgar asked.

"You have the honor of meeting Lord Damballah, the Chief Magistrate of all Justifications," said his escort. "And you, Edgar, are fortunate enough to have arrived in The Realm. At least you're here for a while. Weaker souls, the sheep-like who fell for Christianity's sanctimonious lines, they go to the most dreadful of worlds. It's filled with unbearably self-righteous souls. We look down on them. Well, up."

"So this isn't Heaven?"

"Anything but."

"Then it's the other place?"

"Think of it as the pinnacle of the nether-realms. An honor to be here. There is another realm. It better matches what you called Hell when you were embodied," said the escort.

"Damballah, am I dead?" Edgar wasn't sure he wanted to know.

"'*Lord* Damballah,'" whispered the escort, "always *Lord*."

Lord Damballah's vibration came packed with amusement. "A primitive way to think, although appropriate for a newbie. No Edgar, death is about the only thing you needn't fear here, although those who fail their Justification wish there was eternal death."

"So, what is this chamber, … ah … Lord? And what's this Justification?"

"Here you will be deemed worthy of us … or not." Damballa's vibration tore through Edgar. "We tally your life, hopefully one of accomplishment. The fact that you're here at all suggests at least something in your embodied past attracted our attention."

"Ah, so it's about if I'm good enough," said Edgar.

"Certainly not that. You may think 'worthy,' but never think 'good,'" whispered the escort.

"'Worthy'? Then you mean 'good deeds'?" said Edgar.

"Well … deeds," said the escort.

"Like charity, generosity, church attendance?"

"Most certainly not, fool," thundered Lord Damballah. "You see why I doubt his worthiness, escort."

"Virtues, Edgar," prompted the escort, "… for example, your courage at the trial."

"The trial, yes. An acceptable example," said Lord Damballah. "At least he's shown some merit."

"That can't be an example of good," said Edgar.

"Of course it is, lout. A perfect example. We value self-preservation at any cost," came Lord Damballah. "Self-preservation is a primary source of the Realm's Vital Energy."

Edgar felt a chill for the first time since arriving.

"What is Vital Energy?" asked Edgar.

"The deeds of the embodied create the energy that fuels the Realm of Paradox," said the escort. "Deeds are tallied when the body is shed. One is ruled either to have contributed to or to have depleted our Vital Energy. If enough actions meet our standards, those select souls are invited to make the case for Justification. Just as you have been."

"Though you barely made the minimums," said Lord Damballah. "If it weren't for that trial …"

"He was impressive at the trial," came a vibration from a nearby pinpoint of energy, a lesser entity, Edgar assumed, judging from the thinner vibration.

A chorus of approval followed from other invisible pinpoints.

"What did I do that merits my being here?" Edgar asked.

"Don't be coy; we disapprove of humility. You made the right choice when the other patients lacked your courage. They should have followed your lead."

"Courage?"

"You chose survival while your comrades ignored Loki's offer when he visited. They followed that lawyer like sheep to slaughter. And what did it get them? Christian integrity got them what they deserved - financial ruin," boomed Lord Damballah. "Your hunger for self-preservation showed virtue. You said: to hell with peer pressure."

"You value that?" asked Edgar. "I profoundly regret it, to be honest."

"Honesty. Another worthless Christian virtue," said Lord Damballah.

"Really?" said Edgar. "I pray you don't mean that."

"Silence," thundered Lord Damballah. "Prayer is blasphemy in the Realm of Paradox. Does he know nothing, escort?"

"Show some respect, Edgar. We never use the 'P' word," said the escort.

"But …"

"Why would you regret saving yourself from poverty? The will to survive at all cost goes to the very heart of all we cherish.

That you showed intense self-interest is why you've even been given this chance," said the escort.

"That, and because one of my overseers liked what he saw in you as a young man," said Lord Damballah.

"I regret who I was back then. Give me a do-over and I'd change how I behaved in a flash," said Edgar.

The amphitheater darkened. Even in the burning heat, Edgar felt the chill again.

"There are no mulligans, fool," said Lord Damballah. "I suspect if there were, they'd harm the likes of you. You lack blood thirst for power. If you are unable to present substantial contributions, and I suspect you can't, your Justification is sunk. You will learn the consequences of failure very quickly."

This Realm is madness. They turn ethics topsy-turvy. They see my so-called 'virtues' as what I'm the most ashamed of. He hoped Lord Damballah couldn't read his thoughts.

But he could. "With that, I'm ready to rule immediately," rumbled Lord Damballah. "Clearly you'll never thrive with us."

A dark cloud of another presence fell over Edgar.

"Greetings, my Lord," said the new entity.

"Ah, Prince Screwtape. I'm deliberating over one of your recruits. I suppose if anyone can elevate his consciousness, it would be you. You are dismissed, escort."

"*Edgar Wormwood.*" The new energy slithered to Edgar's side and like a wet reptile wrapped around his soul.

"Prince Screwtape is notorious for effective instruction, Edgar. You'll need his authorization before I encounter you again," warned Lord Damballah. "Although, Screwtape, I have my doubts about him."

Edgar felt the vacuum as the Chief Magistrate departed. The Prince's vibration seemed to wash over him with an echo and a familiarity Edgar couldn't quite place.

"You've lived among the indoctrinated too long, Edgar. My job is to bring you to a more enlightened view … help you align with Realm values. Our standards are classic. They've stood for eons, coming to the embodied in Adam's garden, well before your nouveau Judeo-Christian ethics. The embodied merely mouth Christianity anyway. Their so called virtues never reach below the surface of the skin while ours endure. Open your mind to Realm values … not that an open mind's a good thing."

"But," said Edgar, "my real sins were …"

"… think before you say more," interrupted Screwtape. "Isn't the nature of choice that every decision has a contrasting alternative? Is anything merely black or white? Color itself relies on contrast and shade. But more important than what we choose is the motivation behind the choice. Evaluating intent will be the crucial touchstone at your Justification since Lord Damballah sees your intentions as muddled."

"But, but," said Edgar, "I can't see why …"

"...Enough babble." Prince Screwtape stopped him. "I'll work with you though your flaws abound. But I fear I'll need more time than they've alloted. Your testimony at Lexamin trial led me to believe our values were ingrained. I'm less sure now. But worse, Lord Damballah thinks you're a waste of time."

"Perhaps I am a waste of your time, Prince Screwtape. From what I see, I'm not right for this Realm of Paradox. In fact, I …"

"*Silence.* You can't even imagine the consequence if they deem you unworthy," growled Prince Screwtape.

8

JUSTIFICATION

Edgar's consciousness dissolved, floated, then reemerged in a smaller arena with Prince Screwtape at his side.

"We'll begin with a mock Justification. You'll see how it's run. I'll help you argue that you've contributed greatly to the Vital Energy."

"Greetings, esteemed fellow entities," Prince Screwtape emanated pomp as he began. "We have gathered here in the Council Arena, in the presence of Chief Magistrate, Lord Damballah," his energy plumed as if an imaginary Lord was present ... "to Justify, or find unworthy, one Edgar Wormwood. To permit or deny him a place among the chosen."

"We customarily begin," Screwtape sent energy Edgar's way, "with the Arguments for Vindication. The petitioner highlights his earthly contributions, thoughtfully and, of course, with spin. Present actions that prove you are worthy of joining the rarified beings of the Realm. Go ahead, begin now ..."

"Well ... I ... I." Unsure how to proceed, Edgar's vibration sputtered.

"History, Edgar, give your history, with embellishment," prompted Screwtape. "Justifications are all about self-promotion, examples that show you adhere to the high principles ..."

"... well, I'm 65," Edgar didn't wait, "... or I was when I passed. My earliest recollection is of growing up in South Carolina where I was born. Later, we moved to Prattville, a small town in Alabama near Selma. In my twenties, I married, Rosemary Bowater. We had a daughter, JoAnn, then grandchildren. My Rosemary died ahead of me, but JoAnn is still ... that is ... among the living."

"We refer to them as 'the embodied,' but go on," said Prince Screwtape. "They want a sense of your values. We know your history."

"Well, my daughter, JoAnn, our only child, has two children. I'm so proud of JoAnn ..."

The vibration the prince released was like a grunt of flatulence.

Unsure why Prince Screwtape disapproved, Edgar hurried to continue.

"My degree. I earned a B.A. from the University of Alabama ... in finance. I worked at Bank of America, first as a teller and in time I was promoted far up the ladder. I became a loan offi-cer, a branch manager, and finally I was made an Assistant Vice President of Loan Administration, one of a mere three hundred and seventy-four of them. Edgar's pride was evident.

"Good. Pride feeds Vital Energy. Boasting is appreciated," said Prince Screwtape. "But when you tell of your promotion, speak with disdain about mere tellers. Lord Damballah will like that you can be arrogant."

"Tellers don't make much. Well anyway, Rosemary and I had a two-story colonial, and I was doing well ... until Olaphane. The pharmaceutical company said my pains came from Parkin-son's. But they didn't ... it was ..."

"... Edgar." Prince Screwtape grew impatient.

"Give me some hint of what you want, Prince Screwtape?"

"I told you: 'accomplishments,'" growled Screwtape. "Actions that radiate your true character." The instruction came like a jab.

"Well … I dearly loved my family…"

"Dammit, Edgar, the point isn't to prove you were another sheep among your church flock," said Screwtape. "Show how you broke from family values. Show us the superior nature of your soul."

"I tried to be a good father and husband."

A blast like angry fire came from the prince.

"… but …," Edgar faltered. "I wasn't always the best husband. There was Katherine Lilith …"

At last Edgar sensed approval from the prince.

"But Prince Screwtape, I'm ashamed of what I did with Katherine."

"Shame? You're ashamed because you finally escaped the inhibited cage the embodied call marriage? Because you felt some passion for a change? Your relationship with Rosemary had gone flat. You felt alive with Katherine. Can't you be thankful for what Katherine gave you?"

"Rosemary forgave me … finally."

"I said 'achievements'," stormed the prince.

"I did end it with Katherine. Mostly because Olaphane's side effects got so bad I had no strength to see her anymore. Then there was the Lexamin lawsuit, Loki's bribe and the trial. But you seem to know all that," said Edgar.

"Yes, the trial! Well …?" Mention of the trial seemed to excite the prince.

"I'm not proud of that either."

"How could you possibly feel bad about it?" questioned the prince, annoyed at Edgar's lack of insight.

"You know I was bribed, Prince Screwtape. I wonder if it's you who had Loki call? Maybe you *were* Thomas Loki? Now I recognize your echo."

Prince Screwtape said nothing.

"So, you know I took Loki's bribe and sold out the others. My testimony was nearly word-for-word what Loki had me say when the Lexamin attorneys cross-examined. I crushed Terry and the other patients. I'm feeling so ..."

"Stop. Say nothing more. I told you to embellish your virtues. Your testimony is the one meritorious thing I've heard so far ... well, and your affair with Katherine.

"Meritorious?"

"You over-think everything. Take the pharmaceutical industry and answer me. Did Lexamin benefit from your testimony? A simple yes or no?"

"They won, didn't they? They escaped civil damages, and the judge let them keep on marketing Olaphane," said Edgar.

"Good, ... so go on," said Prince Screwtape, his vibration pumped with energy.

"Profits are everything to Lexamin, and I helped them make more. My testimony drove up their stock. They didn't care what they did to patients - only that sales increased."

"Isn't that a good thing?" said the prince. "Higher stocks raise everyone's boat. A booming medical sector spikes the economy, creates jobs, boosts employment, keeps prosperity. You have a problem with that?"

"Well, no, but ..."

"Didn't your testimony help hospitals stay solvent and physicians to thrive. The healthcare industry got stronger. Hundreds benefited ..."

"Lexamin benefited for sure, but my motivation was hardly ..."

"... you could have caved to group pressure," Prince Screwtape interrupted, "and then where would you be? Ruined. Did you want to go down for the sake of medieval, Christian ethics?

And take JoAnn down with you? Why pile on Olaphane when it enriched the whole pharmaceutical industry?"

"How about what Olaphane did to me ... to Terry? It killed Ralph. It's toxic and ..."

"... what I saw, Edgar, was that your mobility improved after you took it," the prince interrupted. "You were climbing stairs again, moving like a younger man ..."

"Briefly, but then ..."

"... your support of Lexamin may be your most important contribution. It helped feed the Realm's Vital Energy and tops the reasons you have any hope of remaining here ... it and your affair with Katherine. But aren't you forgetting something?"

"Like?"

"Like when you were young ..." the prince hinted.

Edgar telegraphed confusion.

"... the Leibowitz family?" prompted the prince. "You might recap the meeting."

Edgar's energy sank. "You know about the Leibowitzs?"

"Come on, Edgar." Prince Screwtape grew impatient.

Edgar hesitated, then continued, "Well, it was in the eighties. The Leibowitzs came to Bank of America for a loan. They gave a history of their small tool and die company which had grown from a family business in a garage to a 45-man manufacturing plant that fabricated parts for steel bridge trusses. The technology they pioneered transformed old-fashioned, manually-operated production equipment into robotic machines that were way more efficient. Well, the Leibowitzs came for a bridge loan to get past a temporary cash shortage. Their financial track record was solid ... but ..."

"Go on ... "

"Well ..."

"Did they get the loan?"

"I denied it."

"And?"

"Their business couldn't stay afloat. They'd already mortgaged their home. They lost it, the business, all their assets."

"Which contributed to the greater good, didn't it, Edgar?"

"How can you say that?" said Edgar.

"Look at the facts. You turned down their loan application. Before them, you hadn't turned down many, had you? Wasn't there was something unique about the Leibowitz family?" asked the prince.

"They were different."

"How?"

"Okay. They were Jews."

"And ...?"

"Jews already owned half of Selma," said Edgar. "They ran the *Selma Daily-Bulletin* ... held majority stock in channel 10. Owned too many local businesses. The way I saw it, Jews had infected Selma. Someone had to stand up for established families, preserve Selma's heritage. It fell to me. So I earmarked the money for an applicant with a more traditional background ... and Christian values."

"What's wrong with preserving the status quo?" the prince encouraged. "You did your best to honor Selma's hundred-year-old culture which was endangered if Jews - if any minority - got too dominant. Jews called it antisemitism. But it was nothing more than the selective preservation of Selma's finest families."

"That's what I thought back then. But the Leibowitzs were better loan candidates. Yeah, they were Jews, but they were also innovators and employers. They paid their bills on time. Gave their workers health care ..."

"... they were still Jews," said Prince Screwtape, "an infiltrating minority. You helped brake the Jew's influence in Selma.

Imagine if Selma had become a city where the grand old flag got replaced with a Star of David? That you preserved the real Selma is a plus. I want to hear about it loud and clear at your Justification."

"I regret it." said Edgar. "I don't think like that now."

"You'd better learn to."

"I'm beginning to think that 'good' gets turned on its head in this Realm of yours, Prince Screwtape."

Edgar felt silenced by a blast from the prince. "Careful, Edgar," he warned. "Watch what you say around here. Tradition matters. You once knew that."

"Times change," said Edgar.

"Classic values don't, and you have no idea what's at risk, Edgar. You don't know what befalls those who you fail their Justification. Be very, very careful."

"You keep suggesting there are horrible consequences. What are they? Apparently I'm already dead. So what the hell could be so bad? Frankly, it's getting clearer that I'm not right for this Realm of Paradox. The souls don't strike me as happy, and their energy isn't upbeat. What's so appealing about The Realm?"

The prince ignored the question. "You're forgetting a lot you could tell us. How about your participation in the spring of 1965? The march from Selma. Your attack on the protesters. If you hadn't helped carry hoses for the police, hadn't joined in to heckle the marchers, more of them might have made it to Montgomery. You were a mighty voice in the chorus against civil rights."

"Because I didn't know better. Growing up in Selma taught hate."

"If it hadn't been for you and others of your ilk, the voting rights act might be more vigorously enforced today," said the prince. "Look at the amount of time we'd save if we didn't have to gerrymander and legions of us wouldn't have to stand at the polls in the heat to challenge IDs. It's a drain on Vital Energy."

"Some of us have changed with the times, though apparently the Realm hasn't." Edgar's response came unrestrained.

"That kind of thinking begs for trouble," said the prince. "Lord Damballah doesn't forgive a soul who follows liberal fads. Suppressing blacks, Jews, and brown minorities is an important tradition. It feeds acrimony and fuels Vital Energy."

"I've evolved."

"Lost your way."

"You puzzle me, Prince Screwtape. Your Justification baffles me. I'm not sure your Realm is where I want to be. Forever? I don't mean to be ungrateful, sir. I believe you mean to help. But the souls I've encountered aren't kindred spirits. Least of all your Lord Damballah."

"Toe the line, Edgar, or we can conclude your training, and I'll send you to him immediately."

"So what, Prince Screwtape? Do I really care about your Justification?"

"You don't take it seriously because you're ignorant of what happens," said Prince Screwtape.

"What could be that awful?" said Edgar.

"Fail and you'll know. Those who fail the Justification cannot remain with us."

"No offense, but is that bad? The Realm is hardly Heaven."

"That it surely is not - for which I give eternal thanks."

"How can you say such a thing?"

"Obviously I've made a tactical error in your training," said the prince, ignoring the question. "I should have shown you the alternative sooner. Fail Justification, and you are Banished to the Isle of The Untethered. You haven't a clue what that means, do you?"

"Isle of the what?"

"The Isle of The Untethered. It lies within the Valley of Moans."

♦

Screwtape snapped his fingers to usher in The Great Wind which wrapped around Edgar and threw him off a nearby cliff. He tumbled through blasts of fire until he came to rest on a ridge of black, jagged rock. On both sides canyon walls twisted like a snake, and at their base ran The Blood-red River. A chorus of moans and a smell like rancid meat overwhelmed him. Still reacting as if embodied, Edgar tried to retch.

Along the shores of the river in the Valley of Moans, a colony of agonized, fleshless, ant-like creatures, with tentacles protruding from brittle shells, crawled to him.

Horrified, Edgar scrambled to escape, but the creatures were everywhere. Reaching him, they used him as a stepping stone in repeated but futile attempts to scale slippery, smoldering canyon walls. Feeling as though he'd been shoved through a latrine, Edgar joined their urgent search for a way out. But like the creatures, he found no escape. He fell among them, flailing and shrieking. Tentacles pushed him down as his consciousness failed.

♦

When awareness returned, Edgar was back in the practice arena with Lord Screwtape.

"Oh my God, my God, my God."

"I told you never to use that word. But now you know about Banishment. Consider what you saw. For souls denied a place in the Realm of Paradox roam The Isle of The Untethered.

Forever. There is no appeal. There is no relief in the Valley of Moans. There is no end to time."

The ground beneath them quaked, or so it seemed to Edgar.

"Much thought went into the creation of The Isle of The Untethered. Its architect, Lord Mammon, our wise Prince of Pestilence, calls it 'unattenuated agony'. Mammon's genius is that torture isn't experienced uniformly by the sad souls we Banish. Each among the Banished experiences a horror tailored uniquely to their individual psyche. Among the earliest to join the hoard of Banished, was Prometheus, who stole fire from the Gods and dared offer it to man. He spends eternity on The Isle chained to a pillar while an eagle eats the Titan's liver - a meal consumed endlessly. Only Prometheus experiences The Untethered this way.

"And you've read of Cassandra, bestowed with the gift of prophecy. But because she denied Apollo's affections, that gift became a curse. She sees future danger, even rushed to warn of the fall of Troy, but none will heed her warnings. That's her experience on The Isle of The Untethered.

"Whatever cuts deepest into one's frailties - the most hurtful personal horror - that's how a soul experiences The Isle. And they experience it embodied as one of those creatures. Just like you will if you're not careful."

"Horrible."

"Now you know why admittance to The Realm of Paradox is so valued. Or, would you prefer what you witnessed?"

"Good God, no." Edgar felt like the question vacuumed his gut.

"Then for starters, never utter the 'g-o-d' word again. It's blasphemy here. Never used. Surely not by one who hopes to be Justified," scolded the prince.

"Help me escape Banishment, Prince Screwtape," said Edgar, his vibrations shaky. "I must at any cost."

"Now you get it."

"But, what do I do?" asked Edgar.

"Be the being that caught our attention in the first place. The Edgar of your Selma days, and the man who showed himself at the trial. Be cautious in the presence of Lord Damballah. And when you encounter him, exaggerate the benefits your conduct brought the Realm. Embellishment isn't merely permissible here, it's good form. Boastfulness. Braggadocio."

"I ..."

"... as it stands," the prince interrupted, "Lord Damballah doubts you. But I know your past. I believe in you ... provided you can cast off that veneer of Christian indoctrination. It's not who you really are. You used to know better. Your only hope to save yourself from The Isle is to quickly realign with those values. Open to the dark. I'll ask to Lord Damballah for more time and I've arranged tests, to prove your worth."

"Tests?"

"Excursions that reveal how Realm-worthy you really are."

9

A GRANT OF TIME

Adiverse group of souls listened attentively as Lord Damballah led a meeting.

"Next is a request from Prince Screwtape to postpone the Justification of Edgar Wormwood. To delay the deposition of the petitioner," said the Chairman.

"Why wait?" voiced a presence.

"Prince Screwtape sees potential in Wormwood although I do not. Screwtape wants more time to work with him. I'm inclined to banish him now."

"I'm of a similar mind, Lord Damballah," voiced another. "I don't see that our values are instinctive to Wormwood. I fear Christianity has rooted."

"My sense too," said another.

"I've encouraged you to never lose hope that a soul can find the dark," said Lord Damballah, "but Wormwood seems to regret his better moments; his performance at the trial ... his Selma and his banking days. I don't see that he's worth more time, and I'm ready to write him off."

"Roman Catholic, wasn't he?" asked a presence.

"Their beliefs can be so ingrained," noted another.

"Our records show consistent church attendance in his early years and again late in life. Although we found an encouraging gap in church-going as a middle-aged man. A red flag, however, is that Wormwood's attendance often exceeded the perfunctory period of Easter and Christmas."

"It might be nothing more than social compliance. But what if he's taken church doctrine to heart," warned another.

"There's his reverence for that Father Angelos," said another.

"I usually support requests from Prince Screwtape," came another presence, "but the fact is that with things among the embodied so encouraging - with Wall Street spiking, the drug trade flourishing, white cops shooting blacks without recourse, women fondled randomly, and especially with so many congressional representatives expected here soon, don't we have legions to choose from far better qualified than Wormwood? I say 'nay' to Screwtape's appeal."

"While I can't disagree," said Lord Damballah, "Prince Screwtape insists he finds insecurity, intolerance, and greed properly seeded in Wormwood."

"With respect, Lord," voiced a spirit, "Prince Screwtape has been wrong before."

"He has," came another spirit, "but more often than not he's been right. Let us never forget it was Screwtape who discovered Prince Mammon. You may recall we'd intended to give Mammon a thumbs down until Prince Screwtape stood for him. Look what the Realm would have lost had we ignored Screwtape's appeal. Prince Mammon might never have evolved into our powerful Prince of Pestilence. There might never have been The Untethered. Give Screwtape time to test him, and allow Wormwood time to show he's as dark as Screwtape believes."

"Then it shall be so," thundered Lord Damballah. "Now let us move on."

10

CONGRESSIONAL APPROVAL

Edgar stood with the prince on a pitted, stone precipice. Concentrating on the horizon, Prince Screwtape willed The Great Wind to roar in. It encircled Edgar, wrapping him in a cloak of dust and rain. The wind cost Edgar his footing, threw him aloft, then bulleted him through a dark galaxy, past streaks of random stars splayed like brilliant splatter. Edgar, shaken, needed all he could muster to hold it together as he sped through the horizon. In time, the turbulence settled, and Edgar reassembled in human form. Back in the physical dimension, among the embodied, he enjoyed the pleasing feel of arms, legs, flesh, and the familiar sense of time passing as it always used to.

His eyes blinked open, revealing a dozen men dressed like himself, seated around a polished, oblong conference table. A brass plaque in the center of the conference table read:

> *U.S. House of Representatives*
> *Permanent Select Committee*
> *On Intelligence.*

Meeting attendees were uniformly dressed in gray suits, with white shirts and red-striped power ties. The exception was a lone woman, in a maroon suit. Chairman Gilmore Reed was midstream in an opinion as Edgar's consciousness took hold.

"… obviously we remain vulnerable if we allow North Korea to continue providing Al Queda with uranium-235. A week doesn't pass that we're not threatened by some tribal terrorist who hopes violence against America will keep his people loyal. Since North Korea continues to supply them with uranium, our best option is to liquefy the North's armament facilities … now, while we can."

Chairman Reed turned to his right. "General Albertson, you estimate a seven-month window before short-range missiles from south of Hamkyeng Province could reach the mainland. If we strike now, though the regime will retaliate, merely Hawaii is at risk. And that assumes North Korea's rudimentary technology can reach the island. If they can, the collateral damage is unavoidable. But they can't reach the mainland, so California and …"

Congresswoman Shelby interrupted, "…so Chairman Reed, we're to abandon the diplomatic efforts you supported last meeting? We're to give up sanctions that have proven so effective, sanctions our allies unanimously support? Even the Chinese haven't interfered as several of you here predicted they would." She glanced around the table for effect. "You read the same reports I do. North Korean food inventories, rice especially, are extremely low. There's growing unrest in the northern provinces. Intelligence advises that the 'Dear Leader' himself is unnerved. So why is war our best move? Stay with sanctions - the safe tactic that's working. And, Chairman Reed, is it really that easy for you to write off Hawaiian Americans as 'unavoidable collateral'? Is that who we are, gentlemen? Do I also have to remind you of the substantial tax income we get from that vacation paradise?"

Edgar leaned forward, about to support Shelby's opposition. *Despite the contributions Chairman Reed promised my campaign reelection committee, I don't know if I can support a war.*

Hovering unseen, Prince Screwtape anticipated that Edgar was wavering. *I only hope Lord Damballah's attention is focused elsewhere,* thought the prince. *It won't bode well if he knows Edgar instinct is to support sanctions when war is an option.*

The prince pierced Edgar's mind with an indelible image. He emblazoned a panorama of the Isle of The Untethered: a scene of torrid fires; rancid air; and the putrid, Blood-red River, with banks teaming with doomed inhabitants.

The vision stunned Edgar whose hands shook uncontrollably. He held tight to his chair arms. When he regained composure, he rose.

"DDDebate. Deliberate. Delay. Unacceptable!" The force of his growing conviction surprised him. "It's obvious Chairman Reed is right. This is no time for timidity. It may already be too late. We need to act, and give 'em all we got."

Bathed in dark overhead, Prince Screwtape shot an approving vibration.

"Kim Jong-un is as unreliable as the terrorists he sells to," continued Edgar, "and today, my colleagues, I give you irrefutable proof of his treachery. I have here," Edgar dramatically slapped a stack of folders on the tabletop, "the results of my subcommittee's exhaustive study on the heretofore unmasked activities of the 'Dear Leader.' My reports confirm beyond a doubt, that North Korea continues underground preparations for war. Intelligence reports Kim Jong-un is unsure of the loyalty of his generals. He's killed a score of them, but he believes only war will consolidate his hold on the rest."

"But…" Congresswoman Shelby rose to counter …

"...no buts," Edgar drowned her out. "Facts are stubborn, Shelby, and my subcommittee's report," he pointed to the folders, "is conclusive. Our nuclear superiority can't protect us indefinitely. Everyone in this room, even you, Shelby, knows that if we wait, we lose the advantage, while safety is only assured if we strike first."

"... safety for some," countered Shelby, "that is if you aren't a Hawaiian American or a U.S. soldier along the 38th parallel. It's a sure win so long as fallout that blows East doesn't turn the bones of our grandchildren brittle. The 'collateral damage' you euphemistically speak of is nothing less than irresponsible callousness. Have you thought this through, Reed and Wormwood? The rational options are diplomacy and sanctions."

"Too much pontification. Too little action, Shelby," said Edgar. "This is no time to equivocate."

As the words came out, Edgar envisioned the future he was supporting - Korea following a second Korean war. He imagined Seoul, a crater of ash, black silhouettes and torn lumber, a moonscape of cement shards with bodies stacked in streets ... an American-produced Chernobyl in a highly populated city.

Prince Screwtape lit with delight while Edgar held the floor. *Not only has Edgar supported war forcefully,* the prince concluded, *but Edgar's invention ... those reports confirming Kim Jon-un's war preparations ... that was brilliance. Edgar took a risk. Had even a single committeeman asked to study the reports, seen that the pages inside the tan folders were blank, Edgar would have been unmasked. But no one did, and thanks to Edgar, they'll go all out for war.*

Edgar stared at his folders, absorbing what he'd done.

"Nice job, Edgar," Chairman Reed pulled him aside as the committee disbanded. "I'm meeting the lobbyists tonight about your super PAC. Your finance worries are over."

I know what I've done is awful, but perhaps when I'm re-elected I'll propose reconstruction funding for Hawaii. No matter what, I'm better off creating Armageddon than being Banished. There's no way I could handle eternity with those creatures.

He gathered up the unopened folders as his consciousness faded.

◆

In an instant, Edgar and Prince Screwtape were back in the practice arena.

"Your inventiveness impressed me," said Prince Screwtape. "That claim to have details of secret war preparations. I could not have done better myself. I thought you'd be a quick study, Edgar, when I saw your passion for self-preservation at the trial. Now I find an unexpected talent for manipulation. I'm feeling more positive about your Justification."

"It was a complete lie, Prince Screwtape ... and the casualties ... radiation lingers for generations…"

"...a long-lasting contribution to the Vital Energy, Edgar. Wars are a treasure chest for the Realm ... have been since the crusades. You showed courage by taking that chance. *History is shaped by souls who dare to risk,*" to quote a Lord Damballah classic."

"But look what ..."

"Though your fate is by no means secure."

"I thought what I did would ..."

"...we're done for today. Let what you've learned sink in."

"Still I hoped ..."

"Relax, Edgar. I need to report to Lord Damballah. When he learns of the war, hopefully he'll feel less inclined to Banish you, and I have a second excursion planned. My tests become considerably more difficult."

As Prince Screwtape's presence dissolved, Edgar felt a rush of hot blood … where in fact there was none.

♦

Prince Screwtape met briefly with Lord Damballah to describe the next test.

"Interesting, Screwtape. Inventive as usual."

"Will that be all, sir," asked the Prince, ready to leave.

"Actually no, Screwtape. I have a requirement."

"Lord?"

"I don't want you to send Edgar back in a familiar embodiment. I don't want him tested as Edgar Wormwood. Having him arrive in a familiar persona makes it too easy for him to respond by rote. Test him in the body and persona of a person he doesn't know. He can share consciousness with his new persona, but he won't be able to rely on Edgar Wormwood's habits. How he acts will better reflect who he is at the core. Then if he shows Realm values, if we see that he enjoys inflicting pain, that he's quick to sacrifice others for his own needs, if those virtues come easily, I'll reconsider my opinion."

"I understand, Lord Damballah."

"Then get to it."

11

THE VIRTUE OF LUST

Though he tried to repress them, horrendous images of scenes of the Banished ripped through Edgar's consciousness. He could not avoid the images of the eternally damned that Prince Screwtape forced him to watch - colonies of the sterile, wingless creatures with vacant eyes that wandered The Isle of The Untethered without destination.

The chorus of their moans penetrated, and left Edgar feeling like he'd acquired flesh and blood again but lacked all nerve control. It was as if he had limbs that shook and knees that knocked as the screams from the condemned fell on him like a dense cloud. That sense of limb was metaphor of course, his psychological translation of fear. For in the Realm of Paradox the unembodied had no knees to knock, nor hands to shake, nor ears to hear.

Edgar reflected on the final weeks before he'd passed. After the trial, he'd become numb; felt dead even before his death. He couldn't look at JoAnn. *Did she feel differently about her dad? If so, mercifully she hadn't shown it.*

Over and over came the memory of descending the courthouse steps with the others. He'd tried to stand tall, to pretend he didn't see friends turning away in disgust. Doubtless Loki had visited them too, so they knew why he did it. They'd had the courage to turn Loki down. *Maybe I can earn their forgiveness*

- atone with deeds for what I did. I could call Attorney Thaddaeus and recant? He certainly hadn't lived up to the man he hoped he was.

That was also true about the affair. His guilt about Katherine was bone deep. Memories of their affair surfaced at inopportune moments. He recalled the look on Rosemary's face the night she finally confronted him; he'd slipped through the front door to find her waiting up. He tried lame excuses about late nights at the bank. But the hurt in Rosemary's eyes didn't dim until they flashed with anger. She confronted. He confessed. She threatened. He followed with a string of frightened promises if she'd only stay. He would reform. But well-intentioned and his remorse heartfelt, he didn't alter his behavior. The affair with Katherine continued, a cycle of lust and shame repeated weekly. That his ever loyal Rosemary continued to wait for him to end it only made the guilt anchor in his marrow.

Driving home after midnight through streets with little traffic, he'd wondered if Katherine was an addiction. *Was it worth feeling this bad?* During sex, his body seemed almost to vibrate, the explosion completely enveloping when he let go. But he finished so quickly, and the intensity dissipated so fast. And always following sex - came the hollow feeling and the urgency to leave. If only the excitement lasted as long as his disgust.

Yet despite the emptiness that inevitably descended, his hunger for Katherine would build again, and Edgar would be back with her the following week. And the week after that.

When he finally ended it, announcing his intent to Katherine, after her tears and flailing fists, and the slamming of her bedroom door when he left, he was surprised to discover an emotion he had not unexpected: he was furious. *After all, wasn't Katherine a fellow conspirator? Hadn't she tempted me, invited me to her apartment, helped me pick restaurants where we wouldn't be seen. It wasn't as if she didn't know about Rosemary, and that I had a daughter, JoAnn.*

He was done. And, in fact, for years following that final night with Katherine (and even postmortem), Edgar kept his vow to Rosemary and remained faithful. Weeks became months and he began to feel better about himself, the man he'd become, the evolving Edgar Wormwood.

Of course there were moments when he thirsted for novelty, for sex with someone unfamiliar. *It's only human,* he assumed. And when passing a woman with nicely-shaped legs at a mall, he'd strip her, imagine her naked, wonder as they passed, if her breasts were as firm as they looked, how they'd feel cupped in his hands, his fingers teasing her tit. He'd see himself lowering between her legs.

It was only fantasy, Father Angelos assured at confession. As long as he kept his urges in check, and continued to honor his vow to Rosemary, God would think no less of him. In time, thanks to Father Angelos's comforting explanation, Edgar could accept those urges as normal and feel okay about himself … reformed … a better man. He'd leave confession with the good Father like a Sunday parishioner uplifted by the sermon.

Until, that is, like a blast of chaos, came Prince Screwtape to explain that Edgar had it all wrong. That infidelity is a virtue and breaking his vow would show strength. The prince would have him reverse all the commandments, and he'd better listen. If he didn't, well, the prince's raised brows were ominous.

That look became the sword of Damocles for Edgar. To please the prince and not incur Lord Damballah's penetrating stare meant success at his Justification; an escape from that horrible netherworld of The Untethered. He had to try to alter his thinking, squelch ethical forethought, mimic the spineless creature who impressed the prince by advocating war at the Intelligence Committee meeting.

He knew why he'd failed himself. Again. It was terror that drove his compliance. *Those images. Was there no way to avoid them? Wasn't there some way to escape The Isle yet not obey Prince Screwtape?*

I'll take oxycodone - enough pills to send to oblivion how bad I feel about the choices I'm making. Yet that plan isn't viable. Obviously, since in The Realm of Paradox, where existence is bodiless, what good is a drug?

He considered the other popular earthly route to escape.

Suicide. I'll take my life. Isn't that a better choice than Banishment? But suiciding is to think in earth-terms again; not a real option. How do I terminate existence when I'm already dead? Even death offers no hope.

But, by his own admission, the ways he came up with were pathetically earth-bound solutions.

12

TEAM PLAYER

Edgar tried to baffle the screams that came from The Valley of Moans.

"Fail and you'll join that chorus," Prince Screwtape said as he approached.

"Don't let him Banish me. I beg you."

"That's up to you. Start acting like a true soul of the Realm."

"I will, sir. I surely will," said Edgar.

"Which brings me to your next journey," said the prince.

"Where are we going?"

"*We* aren't going anywhere. You're on your own."

"Will I be back among the embodied?"

"You will, but it won't be to Washington. It's a very different kind of journey."

The prince beckoned The Great Wind which swept Edgar above the Valley of Moans and rocketed him into a dark void, beyond arrays of galaxies. His journey progressed through a luminescent path of stars and broke the barrier of time. He felt less anxious now. *I'm becoming accustomed to how Realm souls travel.* As the gray of space blackened, Edgar lost consciousness.

◆

He awoke, blinking to get his bearings, aware he was sitting on a wooden bench in a long room lit by florescent lights. At the far end there were whirlpool tubs, massage tables and wooden stands stocked with barbells. *A locker room*, he assumed, confirmed by rows of uniforms on hangers. Floor-to-ceiling mirrors covered the walls.

His reflection in the mirror was confusing. Though alone in the room, there was a stranger in the mirror seated on the bench where he sat. Edgar stared, transfixed, and began to see himself through the stranger's eyes, experiencing a duality he'd never known and wasn't prepared for. *How can I be two people at once?* He moved his right arm, then drum-rolled his fingers. The stranger in the mirror moved his right arm, then drum-rolled his fingers.

It's as if we're one, Edgar concluded. *I'm the stranger in the mirror and he's me.* Yet the stranger didn't look like him. *Odd, I feel like a child walking in a grownup's shoes.*

The stranger was young; Edgar placed him in his mid-twenties. He was tall and broad with wild, highlighted dreadlocks that ended at his shoulders by an untrimmed beard. Edgar swiveled his head. The stranger's dreadlocks twirled in the mirror.

Edgar's sense of his own body faded as his consciousness flowed into the stranger's. He could no longer determine the boundary of where he ended and the man in the mirror began. He felt the bulge of muscles beneath the his sports jersey. He'd become the body, the personality and the consciousness of the stranger. Yet a blurry sense of 'Edgarness' remained in the background, like a witness.

"Yo EJ." A teammate entered the locker room and tied his shoelaces on the bench. Others followed, mulling about. Lockers bore nameplates, and the one on his own locker read: EDGAR-JAY NERGAL "EJ".

So I'm 'EJ'. Edgar-Jay Nergal.

"EJ." Another teammate greeted him.

And then, as if from memory, he knew why the energy in the room was intense.

This was the day. The one they'd lived for. In minutes they'd be taking the field for the final round of the NFL conference playoffs. His team, the Chicago Titans, were 4-to-1 favorites to beat the Orlando Ravens and capture their division. If so, the next stop would be the Super Bowl.

Getting here had been the hard part. For months, EJ and his teammates arrived at the field before sunrise to drill for hours: monkey-rolls, 50-40s, bear crawls, wind sprints to convert muscle power to acceleration. They pushed themselves past exhaustion, ignored throbbing pain, ran sometimes on little but will alone. When their field work was done, it was back to the training room to bench press for bulk.

iPads had glowed with diagrams as the coaches reviewed assignments, staying until each player knew the movements of every other guy on the offense, the defense or their special team. And when they thought they had it down pat, the assistant coaches returned to drill them again.

They held practice in thick humidity and on bone-cold winter mornings. They ate together, rode on buses and planes together, helped each other work through injuries - whatever it took to make the playoffs.

There'd been days when Coach Brattlestead screamed at them. But they also knew how he battled the owners to get them better contracts. Coach pressed for new facilities and waited years for draft picks to fill weak links. At last they'd become the team ESPN described as, "brimming with talent."

There was running back Dion "bullet" Peterson, and 'Bull-dozer' Romanowski, the outside linebacker who intimidated opponents until they dreaded to blitz. Jay Washington, defensive tackle, destroyed the running stats of the best defensive linemen in the NFL. Offensive guard, Fritz Altuna, routinely opened holes for his backs, earning the nickname "The Wall," for the protection in the pocket he gave his quarterback. Finally there was EJ, Edgar-Jay Nergal, tight end and former Heisman trophy winner. Known to catch passes thought impossible for a mere mortal, he seemingly scooped them mid-air on fingertips, even as he fell backwards, but kept his feet inbounds.

The Chicago Titans reached today's playoff game with an impressive 11-1 record. Oddsmakers favored them to beat the Orlando Ravens, and to be the first team in Titan franchise history to earn a Superbowl berth. Although Chicago fans feared they might curse the dream if they said it out loud, secretly, they pictured a sky raining ticker-tape.

Surrounded by his assistant coaches, Coach Brattlestead huddled the team for pre-game instructions.

"Today's a long time coming, huh, guys," Coach said. "You played through injuries, ran on swollen ankles." He eyed Romanowski. "Whatever it took. We got past our loss to the Ravens - when the bullshit media said you'd been overrated - that is until we played the Ravens again. That shut them up, didn't it.

"Know why the Ravens are going down today? Because winning's a habit with you guys … built with every ounce of heart you show me. And not just on game days - but at practice - off season - the stuff it took to get here."

"Is coach right, guys?" The team's offensive coordinator jumped up from the bench.

"Fuck yes!" EJ rose, smashing fist to palm.

"Above all, Titans, we're more than guys with talent, more than superstars." He looked at Romanowski and EJ. " We're a team. I see it. Every play has been about protecting each other, blocking, opening holes. It's why the Ravens will lose, and why our next stop will be to get sized for our rings. So, how bad do you want it, guys?" The coach raised his fist.

"Ummmmpphh!" Team members placed palms together in an upward sweep, then turned for the tunnel to the field.

◆

Second quarter, EJ took his position outside Devinwill, the Raven's defensive tackle. EJ dug in his cleats and concentrated on opening a hole for the tailback. The ball was hiked, the two lines collided. EJ hit the defensive tackle low, turning him to the side to spread a path for his running back, Peterson, who shot 15 yards before a Raven's defensive linebacker wrestled him down by the ankles. Officials moved the chains to the Raven's half of the field.

Peterson knocked helmets with EJ. "Nice."

Late in the fourth quarter, the Ravens were up, 21 to 20, after the Titans missed a kick for the extra point. With a minute on the clock, the Titans offense got the ball. A series of downs and a perfectly thrown 29-yard pass from McCord to EJ took the Titans from their own 49-yard line to the Raven's 28. With third down and 17 seconds left, there was time for one, maybe two plays.

In the huddle, McCord called for a pass to his tight end, EJ. EJ was jacked. He moved to the line and set his stance when an absurd thought rippled. *Catch the pass but fumble.* EJ couldn't believe it. *No way. What the fuck?*

A second instruction from Prince Screwtape rammed his mind. *"Do it. Remember. The Valley of Moans."* EJ slapped the side of his helmet, trying to knock out the thought. *Fuck no. Peterson, Romanowski ... we busted ass to get here.*

As EJ awaited the snap, a third penetrating cry from The Valley of Moans pierced. He battled to focus. *I won't do it.* But the cry was disorienting. It took everything he had to keep it together.

The center hiked the ball, and EJ slammed the defensive end, cutting left to get free for the pass. McCord threw a dead-on bullet into EJ's gloves. EJ spun, avoided a defender who grabbed for his ankle. He turned for the goal line as a Raven linebacker dove for him, wrapping around his ankle. The hit sent EJ twisting towards the turf, tugging the ball to his chest. As the ground came up slow motion, Prince Screwtape sent a final, thunderous blast of anguish from The Valley. EJ tried to keep the ball secure. But the bone-piercing scream tore through him. Terrorized, Edgar let EJ's fingers to loosen, permitting the defender to knock the ball free. A Raven pounced on the fumble and took possession. Titans fans scanned for a flag, but there was none, and the game clock ticked to zero. Ravens fans erupted.

EJ knelt, threw off his helmet and held his temples. *What have I done?* Teammates turned away when he left the field.

Prince Screwtape hovered. *It took three prompts before he let his team down? This can't be the guy I staked my reputation on? He's going to need a lot more training, or I'll be the one in trouble with Damballah.*

13

CLASS DISMISSED

After embodying him as EJ, Prince Screwtape decided not to return Edgar directly to the Realm. He wanted to see if Edgar exhibited Realm values if he didn't have advance notice of a test. If he did, the prince could breath easier as clear-cut, Realm-appropriate behavior might convince Lord Damballah that Edgar did belong in Paradox.

The prince transported Edgar to Perkins, Oklahoma, a rural community with a population of only a few thousand and dialed earth time back to 2010.

Regaining consciousness on arrival, Edgar was taken aback. *This is not the Realm.* He looked around, confused. *At least,* he realized with immense relief, *it's also not The Isle of The Untethered.*

He was in a room with a row of windows. His reflection in one of them revealed a woman. *My new persona,* he surmised. *She looks about mid-fifty.* Black arms appeared through a gingham dress with a bright floral pattern. His eyes fell on breasts, lower than he'd have wished, and a belly more ample than he'd prefer. On the back wall, an orange and green pennant boasted, '*Perkins-Tyron High, Oklahoma's Finest,*' next to an '*I have a dream*' banner.

Margaret Washington, fourth grade was chalked in cursive on the front blackboard. *A classroom ... I must be the teacher.* That was the last thing Edgar noticed, as he immersed in the new embodiment.

Margaret Washington sat in front of her students and peered over bifocals. As she was about to begin, the classroom door opened, and Principal Darnell Johns entered.

"Morning, Margaret."

"Darnell," she acknowledged.

"Set for the meeting?" he asked.

"I am, Darnell, but the kids are just fine with their paperbacks. There's too many downsides to iPads."

"You made your misgivings known, Margaret. And you're welcome to make the board aware of them, though they're excited about Apple's proposal. Whatever the outcome, I know you'll adhere to their decision."

"But did you give them the study, Darnell?" She waved a pamphlet from the American Academy of Pediatrics. "Their warning couldn't be clearer. The damage iPads do outweighs their convenience."

"We've been through that, Margaret. Are you starting again?"

"The study's unequivocal, Darnell. Kids use iPads for way more than homework. For Facebook. Selfies. They learn about drugs, and the most degrading sex."

Darnell said nothing.

"And violence. Good Lord, Darnell, don't they get enough on TV?"

"As I've said, Margaret, those are big-city problems that have little to do with Perkins kids."

"Do we want mean kids at Perkins-Tyron? One of the great things about us is there's so little bullying. This little school's an oasis of nice kids. Should we put that at risk?"

Darnell shrugged.

"How about sleep?" She again waved the pamphlet. "Says kids don't sleep as well if they're on tablets at bedtime. Young bodies need rest."

"Big-city noise problems, nothing more. Times are changing, Margaret, and Perkins-Tyron must keep up."

"Really, Darnell? I thought our job was to promote health. Has that changed too? This," she tapped the pamphlet, "says kids glued to screens are less active. iPads contribute to childhood obesity."

"Come on, Margaret, they're farm kids with chores that keep them outdoors."

"And their studies?" She pointed to a paragraph highlighted in yellow. "Testing shows kids retain information from a book better than from a screen. They don't test as well. So you show me why iPads are good for them." She slammed her fist on the desk. "Begging your pardon, Darnell." She unclenched her fist.

"I love your passion, Margaret. But it's the board's decision. You'll have your say Friday. Feel free to make your case. But if I were you, I'd remember you're up for promotion, and it's one of the items on the board's agenda for the week after next. You might not want to rock the boat."

"I'm counting on that raise, Darnell. But ..."

◆

The board assembled in Principal Darnell's office. Several members came especially to meet Chris Whitmore, Apple Corporation's Oklahoma district sales manager, lured by rumors that Apple was giving discount coupons to board members. Margaret arrived early with a stack of pamphlets and a flip chart.

Principal Darnell welcomed the board, covered several budget issues, and then introduced Chris Whitmore.

"Thanks, Principal Johns," said the rep. "Folks, this April, Apple introduced an important tool for educators - the iPad. Like the Apple IIe in your library, the iPad is changing education. Imagine. This little tablet," he held it up, "holds every book in a student's curriculum. Fact is, it can hold all the books in your library."

"Um hum." A board member nodded.

"What's more," Whitmore continued, "Principal Johns updated me on the school's monetary struggles. They're typical of small schools these days. The good news is that an entire curriculum on an iPad costs a fraction of what print books run. And ebooks help the environment - trees aren't cut for paper and no water's used for pulp."

"Aha-huh," another board member nodded.

"But here's the thing." Whitmore gestured with a finger, "and I mean no disrespect, but a lot of children from modest communities like Perkins-Tyron can't afford iPads. That disadvantages your kids. Do we want kids from minority villages to be less adept with technology?"

"Indeed," said another.

Margaret eyed Principal Johns repeatedly. She'd heard all she wanted and was prepared to take on Whitmore with points she'd rehearsed for days. But the board appeared impressed.

I don't know what to do. I've worked so hard for the promotion, and it needs the board's approval. The school's facing enormous budget pressure and they're not giving many raises. I've asked for one for five years."

A vision hijacked her thoughts. It was disorienting while somehow familiar. Margaret saw herself crawling in a deep pit surrounded by hundreds of gruesome creatures with bulging eyes, black shells, and jagged tentacles. They crawled on top of each other and over her as well, trampling anything in their path.

A tentacle shoved her head into the dark slime that layered the canyon floor. She started to retch.

"Ms. Washington? Margaret? Margaret, please."

She shook her head to regain composure, realizing Darnell had been calling on her. The vision had come in a flash, but it left her befuddled, oddly altered. She rose, unsteadily.

"Margaret?" Principal Johns prompted again.

"The kids. All-that-matters-is-kids." She spoke haltingly, in labored syllables, until she regained composure. She looked at the board. "Look at these iPads, please." She took Chris Whitmore's tablet from his hand.

Expecting disdain, Principal Johns braced, hoping she wouldn't embarrass him.

Margaret resumed with a strange, forced smile. "I'll tell you, the first thing that came to me when I saw these, was to wonder how in the world a school pushed to its financial limits, could afford these things. We don't have money for pencils."

Several board members nodded, *Margaret had a point.*

The vision of the pit flashed again and Margaret stuttered. "And ... and ... the... well that's the wonderful news."

Principal Jones looked up from his notes.

"Mr. Whitmore here ... the Apple Corporation ... is offering to donate them. A hundred percent - scot-free. Every Perkins child gets to replace their paperbacks with an iPad. And by the way. We get them too. Board members. Free, not just a discount."

What in the world? Principal Darnell's eyes widened.

"Free?" questioned Bill King, the board president.

"Free, Bill," said Margaret. "Which means the school saves much of the money we spend on paperbacks. On shipping too."

Principal Johns stared at Margaret.

"Yeah, but there's a catch, Margaret," said Bill. "Always a catch, right?"

"That's just it, Bill," said Margaret, "there isn't. It's in Apple's mission statement to introduce their technology in schools, and Perkins-Tyrone benefits. We get them at no cost."

Stunned but pleased, Principal Johns rose and stood by Margaret. "She makes a lot of sense, doesn't she? And by the way, initially this fine teacher wasn't sure about iPads." He looked at her quizzically. "But she's come around. One of my strongest converts now," he beamed.

The meeting closed after the board members voted unanimously to accept Apple's generosity. Afterwards, Principal Johns was dying to pull Margaret aside to ask about her stunning conversion. But instinct told him to leave it alone. He'd accept the outcome happily and not raise the issue.

Margaret left, bewildered, ashamed. She'd let the kids down. What would come of it?

◆

Weeks later the date set to distribute the new iPads arrived. Margaret's class had been studying *The Adventures of Huckleberry Finn,* and the book was loaded on their iPads. But the students had paperbacks on their desks.

At her desk, she turned in the direction of laughter. *Hiram and Lewis, cutting up again.* She shot them a look, a warning to cut the chatter, though secretly their antics amused her.

She eyed the wall clock: 9:00 a.m.

"Class," she began. Smiles, alert faces, and wide-open eyes turned forward. "Good morning, and shall we get started? Is there anyone who has not read chapter sixteen of *The Adventures of Huckleberry Finn?*"

The question was met with shy stares and silence except for Shantell Martin whose hand shot up immediately.

"Really, Shantell, you of all people didn't read it?"

"Oh no, Ma'am. I surely did. Every word. And I got a few things to say 'bout that Huck."

"'*Have*' a few things to say about Huck, remember, Shantell?" Margaret corrected. "Hold off a bit, Shantell, and I'll get to you. Does anyone besides Shantell have something to say about chapter sixteen? Anyone? What is Huck like?"

Ms. Washington scanned the classroom for someone other than Shantell to weigh in. No one did, and Shantell's hand still waved.

"Okay, Shantell."

"Well ma'am, last class you said 'bout character,' ma'am. You said, 'think 'bout character' when we read *Huck*."

"Yes, Shantell?"

"So right off I know Huck's character. He all the time calls Jim, 'Nigger.' You said we never use that word. Now he's on the raft with Jim, but Jim belongs to Ms. Watson. They had slaves, you know. So Huck figures the right thing is to turn Jim in."

"That's right, Shantell. What else is Huck thinking? Anyone?"

Jamar Barns' hand rose tentatively.

"Jamar, how good to hear from you. What do you think?"

"Well, Ms. Washington, Jim's a runaway. And the law is the law. Huck thinks he'll go to hell if he doesn't turn Jim in. So he writes the widow and says to come get Jim back."

"Good, Jamar. Then what?"

"But Huck likes Jim. They're friends, so he rips up the letter and figures he'll just go to hell, but he's not turning Jim in."

"Excellent Jamar, and what does that say about ... "

The door opened and Principal Johns entered the classroom.

"Ah, ... a moment, Jamar ... excuse me," she said. "Darnell, I hope you caught the discussion. Twain appeals to them, and did you see even Jamar Barnes spoke up?"

"Today was the day, Margaret," he said, pointing to cardboard boxes stacked by her desk. "Your kids still have paperbacks? I thought you were ready."

"Did you see what the kids posted from the library computer? It's mean, Darnell. And here we are about to give them iPads so they can post more like that?"

"You were Apple's advocate at the meeting, Margaret, and now you're reluctant again? The decision's made, ... in no small part thanks to you."

"But ... "

"Hand out the iPads and show your class how to use them. I'll be back to see how they're doing."

What choice do I have? Margaret rose, hands shaking. Straining to bring enthusiasm, she began, "Class, Perkins-Tyrone High has something for you today. How many of you know about iPads?"

A hand shot up, Shantell's, of course.

"You have one, Shantell?"

"No, but I read 'bout them, Ma'am. They do everything. Games. Facebook. I'm so down with them."

Margaret handed them out as students passed in a line.

"Push this top button to start them up," she demonstrated. Following her, the students pushed the start button and played with the side controls.

"Hold off a minute, class. Let me show you how to open *Huck Finn*."

"The whole book?" asked Jamar. "In this?"

"Yes."

"This thin thing?" Jamar looked doubtful.

"Careful with it, Jamar."

"Awesome," said William Evers from his seat.

"You can email and tweet, ... so much," said Shantell.

"They're for lessons only," said Margaret, knowing it was a limitation they'd never accept.

She eyed the clock. "For next time, move on to chapter seventeen of *Huck Finn*. We'll talk about it Tuesday. Before the bell rings, does anyone need more help?"

"I'm not sure how to get to that chapter, Teacher Washington," said William Evers.

"I can help him after class," said Shantell.

"Nice of you, Shantell," said Margaret reluctantly.

◆

Months passed since Edgar's departure. On a Wednesday, Margaret's class assembled to cover the final chapter of *Huck Finn*. The noise level before class was low, with little chatter and no laughter. Students sat captivated, touch-turning pages and typing on virtual keyboards. Lewis and Hiram tapped their screens. Another played solitaire, and one emailed. Shantell, a fan of Facebook, sent a threatening reply after a post from Jamal.

◆

The class broke for recess. Only minutes into the break, the playground monitor rushed Hiram to the school nurse with a gash over his right eye that required stitches. Hiram had called Lewis a 'queer,' and Lewis picked up a stone and slammed Hiram's forehead. A group of girls taunted Shantell, chorusing that she was a freak. They didn't want her to jump rope with them, which left Shantell alone on the sidewalk.

Margaret watched from her classroom window, setting down the *Journal*, Perkins County's oldest newspaper. Today's unusually large headline read:

STUDENT WOUNDED
IN STADIUM SHOOTING

Below that lead was one more typical of the community - a report that the school district was still looking to hire a bus driver.

Margaret left school later than usual at the end of a long, tiring day. *Nice that I have a bit of luxury to enjoy on my ride home.* Dion's *My Heart Will Go On* filled the car as she turned up the stereo in her new Buick.

♦

Edgar reflected on the decisions he'd made as Margaret.

I never wished to hurt those kids. I knew how fast they'd get lost in their screens. Drown in iPads. That before long they'd be isolating themselves with iPhones. If only books were that addictive.

When I planned what I'd say to the board, my goal was clear. Shelter the kids from technology. Keep them innocent. I was prepared to fight.

Then Darnell threatened my promotion. I needed it. In some corner of my mind the stand I should have taken was clear - even as I surrendered my willingness to take it. But the screams from those creatures! My determination ran off like a frightened animal and a caricature of myself spilled words that supported iPads. It wasn't me. Yet it was. It happened so fast. That's how it was on the field when, as EJ, I gave up the ball.

The Lexamin trial was different. Before I took the stand I had time to think about my ethics. I considered and reconsidered Loki's offer and prayed on it with Father Angelos. I chose to keep my home and sacrifice the others. I wasn't the person I hoped to be. But it was the choice I made after deliberating.

Which is why I'm especially troubled about the school board meeting. It was more of a spontaneous act. So what does that say about who I really am?

It's really not the fault of Prince Screwtape, although he does keep pushing. But I made the choice. And now I have to hide how disgusted I am. Pretending to be proud of what I did. It leaves me feeling even worse.

If Lord Damballah knew how I felt, he'd send me straight to The Isle. I can't take that. But my Titan teammates and the kids from Perkins are paying the price.

The record is piling up. I'm selfish. A coward. If how I act instinctively reveals my true soul, maybe I do belong in The Realm of Paradox.

14

NEW RULES

"Lord Damballah." Prince Screwtape hovered patiently.

"Your report, Screwtape?"

"I see progress, Lord."

"That's hardly a report. Has testing produced anything that contradicts my opinion of Wormwood? That he's not worth my time."

"You were impressed by the way he manipulated the Intelligence Committee."

"I'll grant his bluff with the empty folders showed connivance. He has imagination. But fear of The Isle drove him. Wormwood confided to my overseer that he regretted the destruction in Hawaii. If a soul can't appreciate war, what other blessings will they turn from? And in any case, Wormwood was stupid not to hide his regret. Candor is a brake on duplicity, and we'll have none of it here."

"Though Wormwood did advocate for the war, sir."

"You miss the point, Screwtape."

"I urge you not to rush to judgment, Lord. Edgar's fear of The Untethered grows intense. It's thrilling to watch him tremble at The Valley of Moans. Terror is exorcising his Christianity, which was shallow to begin with. The growth of his dark side will dismantle his orthodoxy.

"That hits the core of my doubts about him, Screwtape. I believe the sacraments have gained too deep a foothold. They fuel his confusion about Realm standards. Most recruits adapt to our virtues so easily. But liturgical hocus pocus has corrupted Edgar- the 'body and blood' and such apostolic gibberish."

"I'm resurrecting him."

"You know well how many souls we've Banished because we uncovered tribal allegiances - a stubborn fidelity to Moses, or Muhammad, Christ or Buddha. Wormwood fits that mold - brainwashed by that priest of his. I see little thirst to follow our path. The lout values kindness - loyalty - a desire to turn the other cheek. It troubles me deeply."

"He's further along than that, sir."

"He still worships, does he not? And honors that vow?"

"For now, but my test will prove that's superficial."

"Perhaps, Screwtape. I've allotted the extra time you requested. But heed my warning. Despite your track record for bringing me exemplary recruits, should I find you've misjudged Wormwood, I'll conclude you've lost your edge. You know the cost of losing my trust. Is it worth the risk, Screwtape? If I Banish him now, it will be safer for you."

"A bit of forbearance, Lord Damballah."

"Alright, Screwtape, because it's you. But you know the risk."

15

BELOVED KATHERINE

Prince Screwtape pointed to his bowl. "Damp chips," he growled. The bartender nervously replaced them.

A holiday among the embodied always rejuvenates, thought the prince, *though I could do without soggy chips and humidity. But the basic earthly pleasures ... to taste ... the music ... those I like.* The prince eyed a young woman several stools down from him *... and sensations of the flesh.*

He scanned the bar for Katherine, frowning when he didn't see her. *I don't expect to be kept waiting when I summon an entity.*

A woman with bleach-white skin approached, wiping hair strands off her brow that revealed weary eyes. She took the stool.

"I'm honored to be called, my prince, and always thankful for time among the embodied."

"You're late," Prince Screwtape said, tapping a wrist watch.

"With respect, sir, not yet." Katherine pointed to the wall clock which showed two minutes to the hour. Her eyes moved across the bottles on the shelf as her tongue wet the corner of her lip.

"Arrive early when I summon," said the prince.

"Of course, sir. But since I'm here," Katherine eyed the bottles, "'ya suppose I could ..."

"You may, Katherine." The prince beckoned the bartender. "How long since your last drink?"

"An eternity. I'll have a Cosmo, cranberry juice on the side with a slice of lime. Your summons was an unexpected blessing."

"I don't do blessings," growled the prince.

Katherine glanced around the bar. It hadn't changed much. The wall television was thinner, but little else was different … the same cheap prints of Venice on the wall, though the heavy glass ashtrays were gone. The embodied couldn't smoke in bars now, she'd heard. *Cigarettes could kill you.* She smirked.

"My prince, any chance I could extend my visit? It'd be heavenly."

The prince scowled.

"I'll do anything to stay longer…," Katherine wiped the corner of her mouth with the side of her fist.

"You know the rules, Katherine. Visits must be brief. But you could be invited to return soon, depending on how helpful you are."

"Oh, God, that would be amazing."

"That word is forbidden, even here. 'Prince Screwtape' will do fine."

"My mistake, Prince Screwtape."

The prince closed his eyes.

"How can I be of help?"

"I want you, Katherine …"

"… anything," Katherine moved in closer to offer a better view of her cleavage."

"Not that," said the prince. "Surely not from you."

"Whatever," she shrugged.

"You remember Wormwood?" he asked.

"Wormwood?" She paused. "Yeah. Edgar Wormwood. The little guy. I do, yup. Married, had a kid … a little girl. Not exactly a live wire, if memory serves. Worked for a bank, didn't he? Had a medical issue?"

"I believe you know him better than that. I suspect you recall his likes, his intimate habits. You spent nearly a year with him … off and on so to speak."

"Ah-huh …," Katherine paused to sip. "As an Omniscient, sir, you probably know my time with him better than I do. You know what a little prick Wormwood is."

"You mean that despite the, shall we say kindnesses you provided; despite his promises, you never got that loan from his bank?"

"I sure as hell didn't. The prick headed the loan committee that turned me down. Then the son-of-bitch broke it off with me. Had some lame medical excuse."

"You went from his mistress to persona non grata like that." The prince snapped his thumb and forefinger.

"Little asshole. His wife was the problem. He was tortured about her. Swore our time together was a colossal mistake, and said he'd do anything if I'd keep it from her. I think she knew. Edgar found her going through his wallet."

"She suspected the affair from the start," said the prince.

"Well if she hadn't known, I would have told her. I told Edgar so when he handed me the bank's letter that denied my loan. I picked up the phone, but he tore it from my hand. He broke down in front of me, pleading like the wimp he is. Said he'd pay my rent for a year."

"Which he did."

"Yeah."

"Well, what I want from you is …"

"… anything."

"… to reel him in again."

"What?"

"Yes. You and Edgar. At it again."

"Fuck that prick? And how do you think that's going to happen? And why in hell would I want to see the son of a bitch again?"

"Because I asked you to."

"But screw him, Prince Screwtape? Assuming I even could I'd rather fuck a rattlesnake."

"That can be arranged, Katherine."

"Come on, sir. You know what he said when he left that night. Vowed from that moment on he'd be faithful to Rosemary - wasn't that the bitch's name? Said he'd never fool around again. That I'd never see his face again. I didn't, and I think he actually was faithful after that. I never saw him here again."

"He stayed faithful Katherine. That's the problem. I want him in bed with you and soon."

"Despite my obvious charms, Prince Screwtape," Katherine raised her chin in a facetious model's pose, "I doubt if even I'm that good."

"You've seduced him before."

"Eons ago, and he swore I was his biggest mistake."

"Are you saying you're not up to it, Katherine?" The prince's eyebrows rose to a peak.

"I have doubts."

"So you're eager to return to the Realm? Should send you back immediately?"

"I'm dying to stay longer, sir. I'll do my best. Anything you want." Katherine pressed her breasts to the bar.

Screwtape ignored her gesture. "Then break his vow."

"I'll try, but he was adamant."

"It's a challenge. He honored his vow for years and still does. But you have a talent."

"He's still faithful even in Paradox? Since when do Realm souls honor vows?"

"He intends to keep his, and that's the point. It's why I summoned you. Get him to break it, and there's not much time."

Music interrupted their conversation after a trio took the bar's stage. The lead musician tapped the mic, confirmed it live, then swung his instrument to the audience and began to play, "In-a-Gadda-Da-vida." A low-rent group, they were loud and off key. Katherine and Prince Screwtape could barely hear each other. Eyes glowing, the prince shot the leader a look, and the frightened musician gestured emphatically to the others to cut the volume. Their tune morphed into "The Power of Love."

Able to hear again, Katherine sighed. "I'll do him or die."

The prince smirked.

"How's it supposed to happen? What's the plan? Fucking requires embodiment obviously, so you'll get him here? Where is he anyway? Has he had his Justification? Obviously he wasn't Banished."

"Slow down, Katherine."

"Yes, sir."

"I'll get him here. You come a day before to prepare. You'll run into him here - the bar you both know well. Meeting should look like an accident. Play it up as if fate must have brought you together again. Wormwood's Christianity makes him susceptible to that nonsense."

Katherine made the sign of the cross, then winked.

The prince ignored it. "I reserved the top floor suite at the Dante down the street. Getting him to the room is your job, and after you do, I want the perverted sex you're known for. The night of it. You'll be filmed. I'll have someone shooting from a peephole in the wall. The film is essential for his Justification.

I want lots of positions. Deep moaning - the recordist likes a lot of base."

"I'll try, sir. But how come a little shit like Wormwood matters to a prince? Who cares if he breaks his vow?"

"Not if. *When* Katherine."

"*When*, sir."

"Wormwood's up for Justification."

"So? Let them Banish him. The prick deserves The Untethered."

"I care, which is all that should matter."

"Of course, my prince. But wouldn't I be better prepared if I knew?"

"Perhaps."

"Sir?"

"Lord Damballah assigned me to be Wormwood's guide. Knowing Edgar's past, I believed he had potential. Beneath the primitive Christian platitudes he babbles, I saw a history of self interested behavior, malicious deception and bigotry. I assured Lord Damballah he is Realm material. I believed in his potential and vouched for him. I'm less sure now."

"Does Lord Damballah even care if he fails?"

"No, but I do. If Edgar isn't Justified, my near-perfect string of recommendations is broken. Several souls on the committee have voiced doubts about my nominees in the past, yet my recruits have gone on to become important Realm contributors. It enhances my celebrity. Despite the favorable impression I had of Wormwood initially, I wonder if Paradox values really are imprinted. I caught him mouthing verse like a Christian. You break his vow and help build my case to Lord Damballah that he is worthy of The Realm."

"So let me get this straight. The prick might fail his Justification because you and Lord Damballah think he's virtuous? He's a selfish lowlife."

"I truly hope so, Katherine."

Katherine vigorously swirled the ice in her empty glass.

"Another." Screwtape pointed the bartender to her drink.

"With respect, sir, what do I get for fucking him?"

Prince Screwtape scowled.

"Though, of course to please you is enough, sir. But given how he treated me, I'd see him fail his Justification and rot with The Untethered."

"It will please me. Little else should matter, Katherine. However you will get a couple more nights here - and don't we all enjoy these little vacations among the embodied. I call it 'the vacation from hell,' quipped the usually humorless prince, delighted at the rare pun.

Katherine feigned a grin.

"Of course, Katherine, if you're unwilling - or should you fail - there are places in the Realm even you haven't seen. I trust you've heard how a soul fares if I'm displeased."

"I'm obediently yours, my prince. I won't fail." She gulped her Cosmo.

The bartender distracted them, trying repeatedly to light a candle on the bar. His lighter failed, flick after flick. Annoyed by the noise, the prince glared at the candle. It lit.

"I will break Wormwood," said Katherine. "He's not very firm about anything - or anywhere." She winked.

"Break his vow. You've done it before. Do it again."

"Thy will be done," said Katherine.

"When you arrive the day before, shop for a red dress. Something backless. You'll need to go heavy on the makeup," said the prince studying her face. And Opium. Lots of it. I want you scented and looking like the Katherine he remembers."

"Of course."

"He'll be suspicious of the encounter. Get past that fast. And knowing how he babbles about ethics - his Christian platitudes - expect resistance. He may bring up his vow. But my faith is in you, Katherine ... a deep abiding confidence that goes to the very core of the person I know you are. I trust it ... and your keenness to avoid the Realm's less appealing venues. Which is where you'll hang out if ..."

Katherine's face went ashen.

16

ENDURING LOVE

Prince Screwtape stood with Edgar on a peak above the Isle's Valley of Moans. Anguished screams from below assaulted Edgar. He moved back, unable to stand it, and tried instead to concentrate on a distant star.

"Not a happy place," the prince reminded.

"You're preaching to the converted. I beg you to get me Justified. I'll do whatever it takes," said Edgar. "

"Watch your words, Edgar. We do not preach and will never be converted. But I hope you're ready for my test. You'll be traveling alone."

"It's helpful when you're there, Prince Screwtape."

"I'm not allowed to prompt at your Justification, so it's time to see how you perform on your own. You'll do fine if you keep the standards of the Realm in mind."

"Am I going among the embodied? To Washington or Oklahoma?"

"My journeys are litmus tests of the soul. They're Realm standards because no two are alike. Each is unique in its ability to examine different characteristics of the soul. In this case, I want to see how naturally you reflect Realm standards."

Prince Screwtape's vibration grew strong and cast an immense shadow over Edgar. The prince beckoned clouds and The Great Wind roared in, increasing in turbulence as it came.

It carried Edgar away like a patient on a gurney. His instinct was to resist; to fight for control. But, as before, he surrendered to the gust until consciousness faded to black.

◆

Edgar awoke embodied, remembering again the pleasure of feeling encased in flesh. He rolled his fingers, lifted an arm, tapped a foot, nodded his head. He'd missed the sensation of limbs. He coughed, and remembered the curious twinge it produced in the back of the throat. His mouth opened as he expelled breath and marveled at the body's involuntary functions.

The scent of smoke passed by his nose. A cigarette. It had been some time since he'd experienced the odor. The whiff through his nostrils was pleasant, but unsettling as it moved into his throat.

He recognized the bar in front of him. Near the entrance, two young men, cigarettes dangling from their mouth, eyed him. Edgar nodded, penetrating a curtain of noise as he entered. The sound of a fret sliding down guitar strings mixed with the chatter of patrons. It seemed eons since he'd been here. The bar, a local dive, was rarely busy, Edgar remembered. Yet tonight there wasn't a vacant table nor seat to be had except two adjacent, unoccupied barstools. He took one and signaled the bartender, "Scotch."

"Shelf or brand?"

"Glenlivet?" said Edgar.

"Nope, don't carry it anymore."

"Johnnie Walker Red's fine, rocks please."

Ice cubes cooled his tongue though the scotch stung going down as it would for a first-time drinker. He rolled it around his tongue, and with each sip, the taste mellowed as he drained the glass.

"A Cosmo." The order came from his left. Edgar watched a pair of long legs swing on the stool towards the bartender. Their appeal was magnetic, the voice familiar, but hair hid her face.

The bartender set a martini glass before the patron.

"Where's my lime?" she said.

The bartender placed a slice on the rim.

Looking up, Edgar caught a glimpse of her face and nearly choked. "KKKatherine?" He spit the name.

She pretended not to hear, holding back a smile. After a careful pause, she turned. "Is that you? Jesus Christ, Edgar?"

Edgar scanned for any available seat, but all were still occupied. "What in God's name ..."

"... are you doing here?" Katherine finished his sentence.

Edgar gripped the bar.

"Of all the gin joints ... Edgar Wormwood," Katherine mimicked.

"What are you doing here?" he repeated, frantically eying the door.

"Time off for bad behavior," Katherine smirked. "On a Realm holiday - but I only get a night," she said.

He stared. "I didn't know you died."

"It's been a while since I did. I heard you passed recently, Edgar. You finding it okay in The Realm?"

"I'm surviving," said Edgar. *I've got to get out of here.*

Neither spoke.

Katherine took a deliberately slow sip. "I like it. I fit in; though to be honest," she lowered her voice, "I really love being embodied again. I don't recall liking it so much before; maybe because my life was rough."

"Leaving family behind is the hard part," said Edgar.

"I had no family, and you know that. The hard part was having to vacate my apartment when you stopped paying my rent. Where did you think I would go? I had no income. No place to live. You didn't exactly leave me with options, pal."

"Well you ..."

"I, what?"

Edgar was reluctant, but, after a deep hit of scotch, he continued. "You knew I was married when we met, Katherine. You knew about Rosemary and JoAnn. I never hid it, and I warned you we couldn't last."

"But our connection, Edgar. You talked about it too ... several times ... how much I meant to you ... how much you liked to have me waiting in our little apartment ..."

"I did, but ..."

Katherine's voice raised. "You hinted you'd leave Rosemary. But I'm the one you left ... high and dry. You were the bright light in my life."

Both sat silent.

"You took off without a warning, Edgar. I looked up that night, and out the door you flew. Do you know what that did to me?"

"It wasn't my finest moment, Katherine, but it wasn't my intent to hurt you. And yeah ... okay ... we had something. But I was married, dammit."

"I hated you."

I've got to leave, he thought.

Silence.

Finally, Katherine broke it with, "Still like your scotch, I see."

"And you, a Cosmo with lime."

Katherine's tone suddenly softened. "Ah, what the hell, Edgar. I suppose those days are long gone." She beckoned to the waiter for more drinks. "I'm not here forever. Maybe it's

time we move on. And we surely have moved on, haven't we."
She winked.

Edgar's brow softened.

"Being angry for years has worn me out," said Katherine.
"And I'm long over you … that's for sure."

"Doesn't sound like it."

"Well I am. Let's get over it. Bury the hatchet."

"You mean it? Let bygones be bygones?" Edgar turned to her.

"Why the hell not?" said Katherine.

They drank silently.

"I'd like that if you mean it," said Edgar. "My feelings for you
were real … but I was …"

"… a 'married man'. You're a broken record," Katherine
mocked. "How well I know the drill."

A trio took the bar's stage. Katherine waved to one of the
musicians.

"So tell me," she said after a bit, "when you got to Paradox,
who'd you get for transition?"

"They assigned me to Prince Screwtape."

"Jesus, one of the big guns, huh. Lucky you. When did you
get Justified?"

"Not yet. It's upcoming."

"Oh, really? You better make it. I'm sure you've seen the
alternative. Avoid The Untethered no matter what."

"I must."

"My Justification was a snap," said Katherine. "I'm damned
glad to be in The Realm … especially after I saw The Untethered. But you have to admit, being back here feels great. I miss
embodiment sometimes, don't you?" She rested her hand over
his.

"I guess," said Edgar, pulling his away.

"Two more," beckoned Katherine.

"I shouldn't ... I ..."

"You have to admit," said Katherine, her tongue sliding around her glass rim, "these are delicious." The movement of Katherine's long tongue fired memories. Edgar fingered for the cross worn on a neck chain, then remembered he no longer had it.

"Just to taste again is nice," said Edgar, emptying his scotch and starting the next. His hesitancy melted with the smooth scotch.

The trio began to play, "At Last."

"Etta James, if memory serves," said Katherine.

"She's the best."

Katherine took his hand. "I want to dance."

Edgar's eyes moved down Katherine's dress. *I can't help it. She's as beautiful as ever.* He felt a swelling. *Stop it. Remember your vow.* He clenched his fist as she led him.

He followed Katherine to the dance floor, eyes locked on the rich roll of her rear. She reached for his arms, and after a twirl to the music, smiled, carefully easing him in. He felt the press of breasts on his chest. His hand enjoyed the familiar touch of flesh on her backless dress, and he took in the scent of her Opium. Highly-glossed lips brushed his neck, and his stirring grew firmer. A wavering conscience whispered, *Rosemary.* But his determination thinned against the rub of her hips and the seemingly accidental slide of her arm brushing his groin as they dipped to the music.

They stayed for the next song.

Katherine was aware of his bulge. "It's good being near you," she whispered.

"But Katherine, I ..." he murmured.

"Come." She led him from the bar.

♦

Upstairs at the Dante, Katherine tugged his belt until his trousers slid. She pushed with one hand, and he staggered back onto the bed. Slowly, like a dance of seven veils, she slid her shoulder straps down, one then the other, then her bra, revealing breasts that with help remained firm. Her large nipples always mesmerized Edgar, wider than most and a deeper red. Hungry fingers rubbed them, his mouth fell on them and he sucked, massaging, fondling, encircling tits with wet lips.

He tugged lace panties down her legs with unrestrained urgency and slid her legs apart, brushing thighs as he lowered. On top came the hot, moist flesh as he entered, the pleasure of penetrating, moving in then out in a see-saw frenzy. He let himself remember how often he'd yearned for this, imagined it, and how many times he'd slammed the cage on those thoughts.

Katherine was all about pleasing him, and fueled by scotch, he was all about being pleased … with little thought to satisfying her. He tensed, and then in a barreling, thrilling release he'd repeat that night, he exploded. Katherine eased herself from beneath him, moved to his side, lowered her mouth over his penis, tightened lips and slide her tongue until his hips rose and fell, and he came again.

As the night went on, Katherine bound Edgar, lashed him, and carefully eased him into various positions until, finally spent, he fell beside her in bed. His eyes rolled with satisfaction before he drifted into the sleep of the drunk. Katherine sat up, sober. A wry smile appeared as she leaned triumphantly over his sleeping figure. She gave a wink to the peephole before stretching for her drink.

♦

Prince Screwtape met Edgar at the Valley of Moans. "Your trip went well?"

"You know how it went," said Edgar.

"You were pleased to see Katherine?"

Edgar's chest deflated. "I was not, and you know it. I committed adultery. I broke my vow. I failed Rosemary once again."

"Edgar, you fool, there is no adultery here."

"My vow was to Rosemary."

"Nonsense. Your actions restore my hope you'll be Justified. I'm pleased."

"Well, I'm not."

"We talked about this before, but you don't get it. What you did with Katherine was to break, finally, from another of your absurd conventions. You ignored that pleasure-stifling eighth commandment and a ridiculous vow to a long-dead wife."

"I gave Rosemary my word."

Yeah, and where is she now? Certainly not here. And we don't honor vows. All you did was feast on the passion we celebrate. Lust is a trait we admire. And by the way, Edgar, for a man your age, I have to give it to you. Your stamina was impressive."

Edgar hid his self-disgust, remembering the horrors waiting if the prince saw how he really felt. *Let it be. Get through the Justification, and satisfy Prince Screwtape and Lord Damballah. I can seek contrition after I'm spared The Untethered.* He paused. *Jesus, what if Prince Screwtape just read my thoughts?*

His memory flashed to his previous night with Katherine, hoping the prince didn't notice his impulse to gag.

17

ASSESSMENT

"You summoned, Lord?" Prince Screwtape waited obediently.

"I read the Wormwood report and find your evidence conclusive," said Lord Damballah.

"Excellent, Lord. I was sure once I assembled his portfolio, you'd see him in a darker light. Edgar's history is rich: Selma, his antisemitism, the trial. And his virtue has grown since I began to work with him: the war he caused; the way he gutted his buddies on the football team; his support of dehumanizing technology. One glimpse of Katherine's breast, and that oh-so-pious vow melted in a hot flash. If I say so myself, Edgar will be an asset to The Realm."

"Would it were true, Screwtape. But I find it indisputable that Wormwood does not reflect Realm standards."

"What? Why, my Lord? He succeeded every time."

"Not the way I see it."

"Well of course, Lord, how you see it is what matters, but I could learn if you'd share your insight."

"Edgar's values aren't consistent with Realm ethics. In fact, just the opposite. He elevates Christian love above the joy of sadism. His ethics, that endless string of stifling anachronisms, suggests he's beyond salvation; his indoctrination is baked in."

"But his successes, Lord Damballah?"

"Superficial. You must dig deep to probe a soul, Screwtape. You think you've proven he's Realm-worthy because you obtained a few desired outcomes. But tell me. Did Edgar respond out of the joy of inflicting pain and the pleasure of domination? Or was it out of fear? If you hadn't terrified him with blatant visions of the Isle of The Untethered, *and I remind that I told you not to*, he'd have gone Christian on us every time."

"But ..."

"When he isn't terrified, Edgar's instinct is to protect, not to inflict."

"What about ..."

"... consider the tests in your report. Without your intervention, would he have argued to bomb North Korea or for sanctions? And if you hadn't terrified him with the screams of The Untethered, would he have betrayed the Titans? In Perkins-Tyron, his Luddite resistance to technology would have prevailed. He doesn't value technology's contribution to Vital Energy. Those kids are right where I want them, but Edgar Wormwood isn't. Fear drove his actions. He's terrified, not an eager believer.

"What about his night with Katherine? I didn't prompt him them. And the video proves how easily he blew off his all so sacred vow. If that doesn't show potential, Lord Damballah, what does?"

"I reserve my praise for Katherine. There's a woman who belongs here. Bribe her with a holiday among the embodied and she'd get the Pope into bed. Which leads to another indication that Wormwood isn't worth our time. The fool admitted to my overseer that he's depressed about his night with her.

"Katherine got him to ditch his vow. And her video earns honorable mention - great cinematography. But my overseer further reported that when Edgar realized it was Katherine sitting at the bar, he reached for the gold cross he used to wear. Religion is entrenched."

"But, sir ..."

"That you've shown me he lusts is all well and good, but it's hardly enough to earn immigration. All of the embodied lust. None more than Congressmen, physicians and lawyers - as well as their priests and rabbis. Lust is so commonplace among humans that I give it little importance. The real issue is Wormwood's morality, which isn't truly Paradoxical."

"Sir, I ..."

"I warned that his inadequacies would reflect poorly on you, Screwtape. I've been patient because you're the soul who recruited Mammon, our magnificent Prince of Pestilence. For that alone you deserve special consideration. But when it comes to Wormwood, judgment fails you."

"I'd never be so impertinent as to argue, Lord. But if only for sake of discussion, isn't Edgar's fear his greatest strength? I often reflect on your sage maxim that, *'Fear is the Realm's antidote to love.'* Doesn't fear help us hate?"

"On occasion, Screwtape."

"And during the creation of the Realm, didn't fear lead us to the Crucifixion and Pontius Pilate's role? Fear shows us Christianity's vulnerability - with its *'do unto others'* and *'turn the other cheek'* frailties."

"Admittedly, fear is a path to that kind of weakness."

"And, when it comes to our preeminent virtues, Lord, how often have you said that our fear of domination makes us eager to suppress the meek; that *'fear leads to the worship of power'*?"

"Indeed Screwtape, my adages truly are Realm classics. But those particular insights are most relevant to the Realm's formative days - when we needed a community founded on prejudice to establish how superior we are. And, of course, we needed an alternative to the Unmentionable Realm when Jesus didn't invite us - may he forever remain divided in three."

"… but about Wormwood, sir?"

"It took eons to establish the Realm," Lord Damballah continued, "to weed out souls not of our ethnicity. Immigration run amuck would have lowered our standards. But with perseverance, look at the celebrities we've assembled: Hitler, who never faltered in his heroic fight for an uber race; and General Secretary Stalin's magnificent genocides; Attila, the epitome of rapacity; and Ivan IV, the Grand Duke of Muscovy, who assembled one thousand people daily for slaughter. Would we have the art of drawing and quartering without Vlad the Impaler? And because you yourself recruited him, I can hardly fail to mention Mammon, our Prince of Pestilence. This endless list of notables exemplifies our very nature - a history you know well, Screwtape, but I …"

"…begging your pardon, Lord, but about Edgar Wormwood?"

"Patience, Screwtape, and you will learn. My point is that because of them, the Realm grew to our cosmic preeminence. That's when souls from all walks of earth's embodied began to flock here to plead for admittance. That, and because they became aware of The Isle of The Untethered. And what does that allow us? It gives us the luxury to pick and choose from among earth's most fertile recruitment grounds - the American senate, Vatican officiates - from Russian oligarchs and an endless score of hedge fund managers."

"But, Lord Damballah, with my deepest respect, I disagree. Edgar Wormwood's beliefs are in harmony with ours. Recall his hatred of Selma's Jews, how he hosed negroes as they marched to Montgomery. You, yourself, proclaimed a No Saints Day to celebrate the lynchings that followed. Wormwood's roots go back to generations of men who hate. His father referred to negroes as 'dark clouds.' His great grandfather, Herod Wormwood, fought with the South in the War of Yankee Aggression. That rich heritage is absolutely a part of the real Edgar Wormwood."

"I'd agree if Edgar didn't scorn his heritage. But, he says he's 'evolved.' Calls racism 'moral decay,' and insists he knows better. It's a tragedy, Screwtape, but Wormwood is a fallen child."

"You're convinced?"

"I'm not one for second thoughts, Screwtape."

"I understand, my Lord, of course. But might I offer a proposition that I believe will intrigue you?"

"Proposition?"

"I have in mind a final voyage for Edgar. It will be different from any test a Realm escort has ever conducted. It could well prove the model for future final tests. In any case, it will offer conclusive proof of Edgar Wormwood's true nature - either way, my Lord, worthy or unworthy."

Lord Damballah paused. "I am intrigued. I've never for a moment doubted your inventiveness."

"My test will lay bare Edgar's soul, and I won't be there to prompt him. I'm betting his behavior will eliminate your concern. Either I'll be proven right, or the test will show he's not worthy of the Realm and should be Banished."

"You do know you'll suffer the consequence if this proves another distraction."

"If Edgar fails, of course, Lord Damballah, I'll take your decision without a whimper. But I know his soul, and I'll stake my reputation he'll come through."

"It'll cost more than your reputation, Screwtape. But I approve it, if only out of curiosity to see what you've come up with."

18

THE TEST

"So, will I have my Justification soon?" Edgar asked Prince Screwtape. "I believe I'm ready, don't you?"

"What I think is irrelevant, Edgar. Lord Damballah's opinion alone matters, and he does not think you're worthy of the Realm. In fact, he's inclined towards the worst possible outcome."

"Banishment? Why in the name of Christ would I deserve that?"

"For starters, consider your language, Edgar. You know that name is forbidden, except for historical reference. The problem is that Lord Damballah thinks you remain Christian at heart. Unless you prove him wrong, I fear for you."

"Not The Untethered, prince. I'd rather die … were that possible. How do I prove myself?"

"I have a test. But it's your last chance to convince Lord Damballah."

"I'll do what it takes."

"Let's talk about what you need to accomplish, but henceforth, Edgar, proceed carefully. I've had to prompt you on previous journeys. I wasn't supposed to, and Lord Damballah knows I did and he's angry. He's allowing a final test on the condition that I absolutely don't do that. This one is entirely up to you, Edgar. You've been a guest here long enough to appreciate

Realm virtue. For the sake of your eternity, prove you're fit for The Realm of Paradox."

"I will, Prince Screwtape. Ohhh, the thought of endless time among those tormented creatures … I can't bear it."

"Then start acting like a soul of The Realm. Or you'll join that lot on The Isle of the Untethered."

19

OUR FATHER

A torrential rain pelted as Dr. Edgar Bernard, renowned neurosurgeon and Edgar's new embodiment, answered the knock on his door.

"We're ready for you, Dr. Bernard. Chopper's on the lawn," said the state police officer extending an umbrella.

"I'll grab my case, Kelly."

They ran to the chopper and ducked spinning blades. Kelly strapped the doctor in as Edgar's medical persona assumed dominance, his Edgar-consciousness operating concurrently. The copter rose and sped towards town."

"How bad is it?" asked the doctor.

"Pretty bad. The roads into Evanston are washed out. The quake leveled entire neighborhoods on the east side. Fuel depot's gone, and most of city hall. The aftershock tore off the police station's back wall. Town's a disaster."

The chopper descended to the helipad. Dr. Bernard recognized Mercy Hospital, where as Edgar Wormwood, he was born years ago.

"Let me help with that." Kelly took the doctor's case and the two ran, getting drenched, to the entrance, past rows of patients on stretchers lining the hall to the operating theatre.

Edgar, gowned and gloved, entered the windowless theatre. Its coolness sent a shiver - a welcome change from the heat he was used to. An array of lights gave fluorescent clarity to the scene, casting a shadow over the operating table with an anesthesia cart at the side. A stainless-steel tray held carefully placed sterile instruments. Monitors glowed, tracking heart and respiratory rates. A pulse oximeter lay ready to check blood oxygen.

Edgar's team had been waiting - the anesthesiologist, the operating department practitioner and the nurses. He turned to Monique, the triage nurse he'd known for years.

"Who was the family they just led out?"

"They were among the first patients here after the quake - before the EMTs started bringing the more serious trauma cases. Only minor cuts. The mother needed stitches on her shoulder for a shattered glass wound. I cleaned and bandaged scrapes on her girls. Nothing serious."

"How many are there waiting? he asked. "Every stretcher had someone. You'll bring me the worse first, of course." Even as he spoke, an orderly wheeled in a patient on a stretcher. A man. Unconscious. Lots of blood on the sheet.

"Skull fracture," said Monique. "Evidence of internal bleeding. Concussion for sure and doubtless traumatic brain injury. Maybe permanent damage. This one's rough, Doctor."

Edgar moved above the unconscious patient as a nurse dabbed away blood, revealing his face.

Christ, it's Angelos. Edgar recognized his old family priest. "Was the church hit too?"

"Someone said the nave collapsed in the quake, but no details, Doctor. If I had to guess, I'd say a beam hit him. See here. Traces of wood splinters." She pointed to the patient's right temple.

"Let's go then. We need to stem the bleeding and release trapped fluid."

"Cerebral edema's likely," said the nurse.

"Got to relieve his intracranial pressure, and get the swelling down before it's too late. No time for osmotherapy. We'll go with a ventric." The team drew closer as a nurse prepared the twist drill for the craniostomy. With a hole created, he'd insert the catheter to drain fluid and relieve the pressure.

Even as he worked feverishly, the real Edgar considered his options. Clearly Prince Screwtape sent Father Angelos as his patient. The Prince would have done it as his final test, and he knew what he had to do. Priests were enemies of The Realm and must die. Killing the Father would provide ultimate proof of allegiance to the Realm. Lord Damballah would finally conclude that his soul was fit for the Realm.

Memories of Father Angelos surfaced. The gentle Father had always been there for Edgar, lovingly so when his Rosemary passed. It was Father Angelos who administered the sacrament at JoAnn's baptism and again in the years that followed for his grandchildren. They often prayed together when Edgar needed solace; he'd counseled Edgar following Loki's visit and heard his confession after the trial. But Banishment - eternity crawling with the damned of The Untethered? *I can't bear that.*

I know what I have to do. Father Angelos is old, long retired, doubtless a few years from death anyway, Edgar rationalized. *It will be simple. No one will know. An incorrect angle of the twist drill, an apparent slight miscalculation. A little deeper than I should go. It's a dangerous operation to begin with. But above all, I can't be Banished. I'm only doing what I must.*

The nurse handed Edgar the drill.

20

PARADISE

The air was foul with rancid vapors that trailed the black, ant-like skeletons clawing for a way out. The damned were in an eternal panic to climb the pit's unscalable, slippery walls.

But there was no escape from the Isle of The Untethered, no comfort in the Valley of Moans. Creatures used one another as stepping-stones, crushing antennae and ramming mandibles into hearts pumping colorless blood, shoving brittle heads into foul muck in futile attempts to ascend. Their misery was intolerable, effort was useless.

Among them crawled Prince Screwtape, the once-celebrated and esteemed recruiter of new souls for The Realm, now hopelessly fallen from that high position. It made the ruin of the once-lofty prince all the more delicious as word of his Banishment spread through Paradox. He'd been so sure about Wormwood. He'd judged wrong. Lord Damballah had warned him.

If you could walk safely amidst the hoard of the doomed, not that you would want to, but if you could trail their wailing, you might encounter a creature approaching. One unlike the others in that legion of lost souls - one seemingly unburdened by the dread on every side. If you watched carefully, you might swear you saw a smile on its ant-like face, as if amidst the horror, it was curiously content, surprisingly at peace.

Although it was The Isle of the Untethered and he wandered with the Banished, Edgar Wormwood found everlasting bliss. For by having failed Prince Screwtape and Lord Damballah, he passed his own final test.

21

GRACE

"JoAnn Wormwood!" Father Angelos smiled from his well-worn recliner when JoAnn entered his living room.

"Well aren't you looking good, Father," she said, handing him a bouquet of white calla lilies. "Sitting up, and reading, I see. Your favorite book, I believe." JoAnn winked. "I'd heard your recovery was going great, Father."

"These are elegant, JoAnn, thank you. How nice of you to visit this old man ... and with flowers."

"Wouldn't miss the chance, Father."

"So tell me, how you are. And the kids?"

"Not a lot to report on that score, Father. We're all doing well. I got a promotion at work."

"I'm not surprised. You're a capable woman. What else?"

"I am missing Dad a lot, Father. It's to be expected, of course. But I think of him so very often."

"I can't imagine how difficult it must have been. Finding him as you did that morning. A terrible shock."

"He'd suffered from that drug so long - at least he's free of that. But can I tell you something weird, Father? I'm having dreams about him. Nightly. It's as if he visits while I sleep. They're not unsettling - the opposite really - they reassure me."

"Tell me about them if you'd like."

"They're so vivid ... like it's real. Dad's face is before me. I get the sense he's trying to tell me it's okay - that he's okay. I feel peaceful when I wake up. Loved. As if he's assuring I shouldn't worry about him."

Father Angelos looked bewildered and stared silently.

"You okay, Father?" JoAnn asked, seeing his expression.

"I'm fine. More than fine." He paused as if deciding. "I want to share something, JoAnn. Marvelous because it's so similar to your dream. Since my surgery, I've had the sense that Edgar's trying to reach me. I don't dream it. It's more intuitive - a thought that comes daily. As if your dad wants me to know he's at peace. And he's telling me my recovery will go well ... and it has. I'm stronger every day, and that's not bad at my age. I have much to be grateful for."

JoAnn smiled.

"You know your father was a favorite. We prayed when your mother died - shared precious times."

JoAnn looked into his moist eyes.

◆

That the Father lived through the quake was remarkable. The doctors said his head wounds should have killed him. But he'd been raced to the hospital in time to be saved by a gifted neurosurgeon who'd arrived at the hospital exactly when the Father did. One ER doctor, not prone to things spiritual, volunteered to JoAnn that it was a miracle. JoAnn replied that it was karma, saying the Father's good deeds had come round.

◆

The month after JoAnn's visit, Father Angelos, fully recovered, celebrated his 83rd birthday. The church and many of his old parishioners invited him to deliver a special, celebratory Sunday sermon, and the Father accepted.

Father Angelos stood at the elevated pulpit beaming and unbent above the congregation. He chose Grace as his topic.

"So what exactly is Grace?" he began after his opening prayer.

"I believe it's a Divine influence operating in we humans - a gift - to regenerate us, sanctify us, and most of all to give us the strength to endure trials and resist temptation. My prayer is the hope that you are blessed with Grace in your lives, as I have been."

It might have been with his own recovery in mind, or maybe spurred by a long-time parishioner who whispered through the priest's intuition, but Father Angelos asked his flock to bow their heads and quoted from Isaiah 38:16-17:

"You restored me to health and let me live. Surely it was for my benefit that I suffered such anguish. In your love you kept me from the pit of destruction; you have put all my sins behind your back."

GLOSSARY

DEMONIC NAMES AND THEIR DERIVATION

Father Angelos - *Edgar's priest. Angelos comes from the Greek name for angelic and is the antithesis of demonic.*

Lord Damballah. *The Chief Magistrate of The Realm is named after Damballah, the serpent god in Haitian Voodoo tradition. Damballah rules the mind, intellect and cosmic equilibrium. White rum is sacred to him. Damballa, as the serpent spirit and The Great Master, created the cosmos by using his 7,000 coils to form the stars and the planets in the heavens and to shape the hills and valleys on earth.*

Katherine Lilith. *Lilith relates to an historically early class of female demons, (lilītu) in ancient Mesopotamian religion, found in cuneiform texts of Sumer, the Akkadian Empire, Assyria, and Babylonia. Lilith, the Hebrew female devil, is a figure in Jewish mythology from the Babylonian Talmud. She reappears throughout history, for example as Adam's wife in Eden.*

Thomas Loki. *Loki, is a Norse mythological name for the devil and notable as a shape shifter, who, in separate incidents in Norse mythology, appears in the form of a salmon, a mare, and a fly. Some scholars of Norse mythology describe Loki as a trickster god.*

Lord Mammon, Prince of Pestilence - *Mammon is a worshiper of wealth above all values. He is associated* with the greedy pursuit of gain. The Gospel of Matthew and the Gospel of Luke both quote Jesus using his name in a phrase rendered in English as, "You cannot serve both God and Mammon."

Prince Screwtape - *Screwtape is the fictional demon created by the Christian author C. S. Lewis in his satire,* The Screwtape Letters. *Screwtape holds the rank of Senior Tempter and serves as the undersecretary of his department in what Lewis envisages as a sort of infernal Civil Service. The demon Screwtape is assigned to guide his protegee in proper underworld behavior.*

Jim Thaddaeus - *Edgar's attorney conducting the class action law suit against Lexamin Pharmaceuticals. Judas Thaddaeus, also known as St. Jude, is the Roman Catholic patron saint of lost causes.*

Edgar Wormwood. *Wormwood is the nephew of the demon Screwtape in Lewis'* The Screwtape Letters. *The correspondence he receives from Screwtape, his uncle and mentor, is meant to guide him in the ways of proper underworld behavior.* **Note:** Edgar J. Nergal, "EJ." *Nergal is the name for the Babylonian god of Hades.*

Please go to Amazon.com and give your review of* The Realm. *All reviews, good or bad, help inform readers who will benefit from your comments.

OTHER BOOKS BY THE AUTHOR OF *THE REALM*

Non Fiction

Coming to Terms with Aging: the secret to meaningful time, RDR books

Memoir

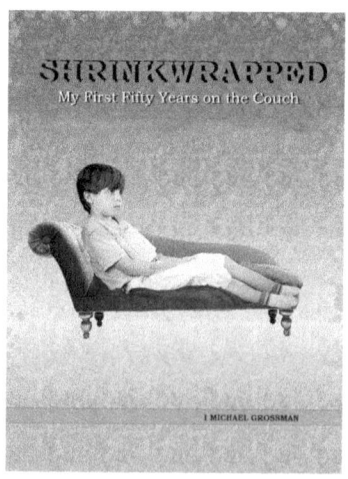

Shrinkwrapped: my first fifty years on the couch, RDR Books

Older Children's Adventure

Mike the Moose: Master of Marbles, Ebook Bakery

Ethical Fantasy/Adventure

The Power, a paranormal fantasy, Ebook Bakery

Poetry

In Disappearing Ink:

poems you can never find when you need them, Ebook Bakery

ABOUT THE AUTHOR

The Realm is the fantasy of I. Michael Grossman. (The "I." is his full given first name - for which, although he was there, he claims no responsibility.)

Grossman has authored five other books:

- *Coming to Terms with Aging, the Secret to Meaningful Time*, originally published by RDR Books of California.

- *Shrinkwrapped: My First Fifty Years on the Couch*- a psychological memoir published by RDR Books.

- *The Power*, fiction, an examination of power and ethics wrapped in a mystical adventure.

- *Mike the Moose, Master of Marbles*, a true-to-life story about a completely fictitious moose.

- *In Disappearing Ink*, poetry titled to reflect the longevity of his poetic fame.

"If I had sense, I'd stick to one genre," says Grossman.

Grossman's articles cover similarly diverse topics written for *Advertising Age, Ergo Solutions* magazine, *The CLIA Cruise Industry Annual Report, The American Banker,* and *Plane & Pilot* magazine.

He holds a B.A. and M.A. from Michigan State University. He taught English and Journalism at Oakland Community College and courses at The New School in Manhattan before leaving academia for what they promised would be the *"real world."*

Grossman founded four businesses. Cruises of Distinction and Office Organix were sold so he could *"go write a few books."* He currently runs MyGreenMind.com and EBook-Bakery.com, the latter, a self-publishing venture helping other authors publish.

He, his wife Susan, and a varying number of four-legged creatures share truly blessed lives in Rhode Island.